To Jo
I hope you wonderful birthday x

ALL for THE LOVE of JOSIE

A Willow Green Village Cozy Mystery

Evelyn Harrison

Warmest wishes
Evelyn Harrison
17/11/2016

Raven Crest Books

Copyright © 2015 Evelyn Harrison

The right of Evelyn Harrison to be identified as the author of this work has been asserted by her in accordance with the Copyright, Designs and Patents Act 1988

All rights reserved.

This is a work of fiction. Names, characters, businesses, places, events and incidents are either the products of the author's imagination or used in a fictitious manner. Any resemblance to actual persons, living or dead, or actual events is purely coincidental.

No part of this publication may be reproduced, stored in a retrieval system or transmitted in any form or by any means including photocopying, electronic, recording or otherwise, without the prior written permission of the rights holder, application for which must be made through the publisher.

Cover Design by www.StunningBookCovers.com

ISBN-13: 978-0-9931909-2-6
ISBN-10: 0-99-319092-8

Whatever you can do or dream you can, begin it

Boldness has genius, power and magic in it!

W.H. Murray, from a 'very free translation' of *Goethe's Faust* in *The Scottish Himalayan Expedition*

As an eleven year old, I remember quite clearly sitting in an English lesson dreaming that one day I would write a book. Fifty-four years later, I have not only written my first novel, but also, I have had it published too. Thanks to Dave at Raven Crest Books for all your guidance.

It's been a long and not uneventful journey of course and I have many people to thank. My family, especially my husband Ian, children Rob, Claire and Sarah together with my friends, Linda, Sally, and Georgina, for their dedication to, at the time, the unedited manuscript and their continued belief in my ability. Lastly, to the young woman who edited my book, Heather Lawson.

PROLOGUE

The responsibility of being a father was one that David Wright took very seriously. It only seemed like yesterday when their daughter, Josie, had come screaming into their lives. His wife, June, had suffered several miscarriages during the first few years of their marriage and they were both beginning to believe parenthood wasn't going to happen for them. Then the joyous day finally arrived and June held in her arms her green-eyed, auburn-haired baby, bringing them such happiness they thought they would burst.

The early years proved a struggle, but as time rolled by, and the family's fortunes grew, life became almost perfect. Of course, they knew she would fly the nest one day, but they had not prepared themselves for the complete emptiness they felt when she eventually left their house forever.

David and June were full of pride seeing their confident, grown up daughter off at the station for university, although they could not help but worry about how she was going to manage all her luggage when she got to the other end.

"Don't fret, pops, I'll be fine," she had enthused and, of course, she was. They always looked forward to her visits home during the holiday times and hearing her tales of university life, although they were more than certain they were not privy to all her experiences.

After two years, they had the phone call that she

would not be coming home alone for Easter; she would be bringing her boyfriend, Maxwell Forrester, to meet them.

"Is this the same young man you were saying only a few months ago was an 'arrogant Ozzie', Josie dear?" June questioned.

"Yes, well, things change, people change and anyway mum, it's not been months, it's been more than a year," Josie stuttered down the receiver. "We understand each other now; in fact... well, we'll talk when I get there." With that, she hung up the phone.

The late Easter was warm with very welcome sunny skies; a relief from the cold the country had experienced during the winter. Josie arrived at the train station with Max in tow. David met them in his almost-new, red Ford Escort, leapt out of the car and kissed his daughter on both cheeks.

"Dad, this is Max. Max, my dad, David."

"Pleased to meet you, sir," said Max politely, in his unmistakable Australian accent, whilst extending his hand in David's direction.

"Likewise," David replied, returning the gesture, gripping Max's hand rather harder than he normally would; David believed he could tell a lot about a person simply from their handshake. Taken aback by this show of dominance, Max smiled awkwardly and released his grip. Satisfied, David turned to his daughter. "Mum's really excited about your visit, pumpkin; she's been very busy cooking all day." David put their luggage into the boot and indicated he wanted Josie to sit in the front with him.

Arriving at the house, they were immediately greeted by the open arms of June, who hugged Max enthusiastically before kissing her daughter.

"Welcome Max, it's lovely to meet one of Josie's university friends. Josie, show Max the spare room, he can put his case in there."

"Do you mean dad's study?"

"No dear, the spare room," June emphasised, sounding a bit harassed. When Josie had told them she was bringing Max home, she had gone into overdrive, instructing David to clear and decorate his study. She also bought a single bed and small chest of drawers, making the room comfortable for this new stranger in their lives.

That evening they all sat down to a beef casserole with dumplings. "That was the best meal I have had since arriving in the UK, Mrs. Wright, thank you."

"Oh, it was a pleasure and please, call me June. Do you have room for apple pie and custard?"

When the meal was finished, Josie helped her mother clear the table before beginning to stack the dishwasher.

"Well, Max seems a nice enough young man," June began, "but like I said on the phone, I was surprised when you told me you were seeing him, dear. I hope he's not distracting you from your studies?"

"Everything is fine; in fact my life at the moment couldn't be better. I love him, mum." She held June by her arm and looked directly into her eyes. "I love him very much."

June turned away; she was never one for conversations about people's emotions. "Tea or coffee, dear? I can make either." Josie realised that this was her mother's way of ending the conversation, so, for the moment, respecting her dismissive attitude, she carried the coffee mugs on the tray into the lounge and placed them very carefully on the table in front of the fireplace. Max was sitting in the armchair by the window and Josie joined him, warily perching on the arm.

Suddenly, she glanced at Max and put down her mug prior to removing a small item from her pocket. "Mum, Dad, we've got something to tell you," she declared, holding out her left hand. "Max and I are engaged!"

David and June looked at Josie's outstretched hand with astonishment; a simple gold band topped with a small blue sapphire was now adorning her finger.

"Josie, oh Josie, this is a bit sudden, isn't it dear?" June cried, seeming to speak for them both, because for once David was lost for words; instead, he rose from his chair and without any apparent emotion left the room.

Josie ran after him. "Dad, please understand - we're in love!"

David turned and looked sadly into his daughter's face. "You could have the world at your feet, why do you want to tie yourself down? You haven't even finished university yet."

"I know what I'm doing, dad, and I know what I want. We both intend to finish university before we get married. Don't you like Max?"

"I hardly think that spending an afternoon with him has given me any indication of his suitability as a son-in-law, do you?"

For the rest of their stay, June and David scrutinised every move Max made. As they waved them off from the station a week later, David exclaimed, "I'll give it six months for her to come to her senses."

The following August, much to the

disappointment of her parents, Josie and Max were married. David's parting words to his cherished daughter were simple. "If you ever need me, I'll be there. Wherever you are in the world, my darling, if you need me, I'll be there."

Life, of course, can be very cruel. Following the happy event, a cloud of sadness descended on the family. Phillip, David's older brother, unexpectedly departed this life, the consequence of complications from a bout of pneumonia. He left all his possessions to his brother, who in turn decided to invest in two properties. First, he bought a bungalow in Devon and then a challenge: a plot of land in Ardres, a village southeast of Calais in northern France, on which stood a very derelict, unrecognisable building he intended to turn into his dream holiday retreat.

Several months after their wedding, Josie informed them that she and Max intended to move out of London into a small cottage, which was in need of some renovation.

"Dad, we've found a wonderful little place in a village called Willow Green, doesn't just the name sound absolutely fantastic?" Josie resounded excitedly on the phone. "We would love it if you and mum would come and see it."

Of course, some people look at things with rose-tinted glasses. They are so in awe at what they think they are seeing, they don't see the negatives. Not see, for instance, the wallpaper peeling off the wall in the front room, the damp patch where the roof is leaking and the space where the kitchen should be does not actually have a kitchen, in any shape or form.

"I don't know what they are thinking, June. There's so much work to be done before they can move in."

"Don't you? Do I have to remind you about a certain French property?" June remarked, without even looking up from her ironing.

That summer David helped oversee the improvements to Brook Cottage and satisfied himself that, when at last it was finished, his daughter would be very happy there – yes, very happy indeed.

CHAPTER 1 – A CHANCE MEETING

Maxwell Forrester bit into his cheese and ham sandwich with little enthusiasm. Usually at lunchtime he accompanied his co-workers to the pub on the corner, where he enjoyed the banter with the Aussie bar staff, but not today – he simply wasn't in the mood.

Sitting quietly on a weather-beaten park bench, snuggling close to the edge of the small lake which dominated the popular London park, he gazed dejectedly into the cool water, contemplating the meeting everyone had been summoned to early that morning.

The Managing Director of Hickmans, Mr. Forbes, had spoken eloquently about the need to tighten their belts. He had promised there would be no redundancies at this stage, but regrettably there had to be cutbacks, namely a twenty percent reduction in pay across the board, to take effect immediately.

With the word 'immediately', resounding from Mr. Forbes' lips, a low murmur had circled the room. Max was in turmoil. With a substantial mortgage to pay and a growing family, how were they going to manage? In anguish, he tossed the remnants of his sandwich into the murky water and watched as two ducks fought furiously over their prize of the small morsel.

Months passed in seemingly slow motion and Max still hadn't been able to summon up courage to tell his wife, Josie, about his drop in salary. He realised soon he would have no choice; for one thing, she was talking about taking a last-minute holiday. How was he going to convey to his beautiful wife and daughters, who he adored unconditionally, that not only could they not afford a holiday but, in addition, they might lose their beloved cottage as he had already been forced to dip into their meagre savings?

The bench in the park was becoming his regular lunchtime spot. It gave him time to think, to mull over his life, away from the hubbub of the office environment. He recalled clearly the day Josie suggested she went back to work, remembered how it made him feel irritated, as if she was questioning his ability to provide for his family.

On reflection, the extra money would have come in very useful. In his world, a real man would make sure they had no worries. He put his head in his hands; what the hell was he going to do? All of a sudden, he became aware of someone sitting down next to him.

"Max? Max Forrester, is it really you? I don't believe it, after all these years." Max looked up immediately and found himself face to face with Antonio Borelli, an old acquaintance from his time at university.

"Antonio? What a surprise, I can't believe it. Do you work around here? " Max asked, just as Antonio leaned forward and gave him an unexpected manly hug.

"No, not yet, in time maybe; I actually have my eye on a few properties. I simply had business in the area today, selling a very expensive car to a very rich Arab."

"So you're selling new cars now? Things must be looking up."

Antonio sat back and smiled a satisfied smile. "Can't complain, the country's going to the dogs, but the Borelli family are definitely keeping their heads well above water. How about you? I hear through the grapevine you're an accountant and married with a couple of kids."

"Yes, how on earth did you find that out?"

"Ran into some friends of ours from uni last year, Stu and Andy, you must remember them, and the great times we had together."

Of course, how could he forget that first year of warm beer and hot women and the way Antonio – being of hot-blooded Italian descent – seemed more interested in the latter than getting down to any real studying. The lucky bastard always seemed to have ladies of all ages, shapes, and sizes just falling at his feet.

The four of them had shared a terraced house on a rather dubious London side road, where they soon became infamous for holding raucous parties most weekends, especially in the first few months; the brainwave of Antonio to attract female company.

He recalled one particular evening when he came across an uninhibited Antonio in bed with two naked women. At the time, he thought Antonio a hero; his own sexual immaturity showing through. However, by the beginning of the following summer, when Antonio had failed all his exams and had been drummed out of university in disgrace, Max wasn't sorry to see his corrupt influence depart from their lives – in fact, to be honest, he was more than a little relieved.

Now here he was, once again talking to this university drop-out, who had obviously done well for himself and was outwardly rolling in money; his dark blue, Armani suit was definitely not off the peg.

"All I can remember, Antonio, was hangover after hangover in that first year and, yes, perhaps a little studying. You certainly weren't a good role model."

"Oh Max, believe me when I say they were good times. Anyway, I managed to get on without a degree – would have gone into the family firm no matter what. Got hell from the old man at the time though; he wanted me to be the first Borelli to graduate, but he came round in the end – even gave me a managerial position. You seem to be doing well yourself by the way, is your organisation around here?"

"Yes, it's only a few streets away." Max hesitated before he said anything else. In hindsight, he should have left it at that and made some excuse for having to get back to work. He should have lied and told Antonio things could not be better, extremely busy workload, promotion in the offing, that sort of thing – but foolishly he didn't. "Must admit, just at the minute, things are a bit difficult money-wise, but I'm sure it's only temporary."

Looking thoughtful, Antonio pondered for a brief moment. "Listen old boy, I might be able to put some work your way. I was never any good at accounts and as our last accountant left, well... let's just say he left suddenly a week ago. We need someone we can trust, if you understand what I mean. Would you be interested?"

Max replied hurriedly, "I couldn't do anything unethical; I might be desperate, but I pride myself that I've always done things well within the law."

Antonio looked indignant. "You've got the wrong idea, Max. I'm hurt that you would think I'd put you in such a position. You're my friend, and if you want work then I could put some your way to help see you through this bad patch you're in, that's all. Say a few hours a day while still staying at your current job. How does that sound?"

"I don't see how that would pan out, I mean, how far away are your premises?"

"I think we can safely say, if I get my way, you won't have far to travel, my friend."

***

That is exactly how the partnership began. Max would work a couple of hours in the morning and then a few more every evening, leaving Hickmans promptly at five-thirty to head out for Antonio's newly purchased offices in Heath Street, conveniently only a brisk twelve minute walk away, for which he was very handsomely rewarded – in cash. Max never asked any unnecessary questions; he felt the less he knew about the running of the Firm the better. He just did what he was asked to do and left it at that, an attitude which Antonio and his family definitely appreciated.

Overnight, his financial worries had changed; the Borelli family were certainly very generous with the amount of money they paid to their employees. No longer fearing ruin, and with his family foremost in his mind, he was determined to make the most of his renewed good fortune, however long it lasted.

Now he had so much ready money, his headache was how to handle it. He simply couldn't deposit all of it into his bank account, or he and Josie's joint account, without questions being raised. At first, he simply topped up the deficit his reduced salary had left, so Josie wouldn't notice any difference, but afterwards he still had literally thousands more a month to deal with.

Then one night, on the train home, he had a eureka moment – he would send the rest of the money home to Australia by opening an account in Cairns. To add to this, he had a further brainwave: he would contact his friend Annie, to whom he had not spoken since he left in '78, and ask her if he could invest in the family farm.

The sound of her excited voice on the other end of the phone brought back memories of his last year at home where, as a young man of eighteen, he had been thoroughly enjoying his life; going to school, playing sports, and helping his dad on the farm. He rarely thought of his mum by then, mainly because Annie's presence had more than filled the empty void her premature death had left. Yes, he loved the idea of being in a position to help Annie.

CHAPTER 2 – A WAY OUT

Although his money worries were apparently resolved, there was an inevitable downside to his renewed prosperity. Max found he was spending more and more time away from home, without being able to explain the real reason to Josie; in other words, he found himself lying repeatedly to his wife.

With the work mounting up in the Heath Street office, he soon became conscious of the fact that the ever-growing accounts Antonio was expecting him to work on had very little to do with selling cars. By the time he realised this, it was too late to back out – he was in too deep and anyway, unashamedly, he was enjoying the feeling the money was giving him. His usual moral high ground had definitely taken a bit of a nosedive.

The office building itself appeared quite a dingy place from the outside, in fact most people would pass it by without giving it a second glance; Max believed its inconspicuous exterior was the reason Antonio had chosen it. Inside, however, was another matter entirely.

Max's set of rooms had been very tastefully decked out; he even had his own coffee making machine, exclusively for his use. Two other, larger units along the corridor made up this particular branch of the Borelli Empire. He had never been asked to step foot in any of the other offices, but he was certainly aware of numerous visitors coming and going, especially throughout the evening hours.

Max rapidly came to realise the Borelli family actually owned the entire block. He speculated that perhaps they had invested in it for further expansion; certainly, the lower floors seemed to be in constant use for storage purposes. Of what was being stored, he had no knowledge, but he had seen lorries loaded with crates arriving and leaving on several occasions.

He hadn't been working there very long before he was introduced to Antonio's brother, Marco. Max sensed he was an unsavoury character from the minute they met. Not only was he shorter than Antonio was in stature, but also in his manner. He carried an air of arrogance about him that Max felt would intimidate most men, and every time he entered Max's office, a strong aroma of Brut aftershave seemed to linger long after he had left the room. Marco made him feel uneasy; Max decided he was certainly not the sort of individual anyone would want to meet in a dark alleyway, alone, at night.

On the other hand, Candy – Antonio's long-term girlfriend – a gorgeous hazel-eyed, blonde-haired woman, was like a breath of fresh air. She had an innocent way about her, which Max found very appealing – she would often pop into Max's office to have a chat while Antonio was doing business next door.

Time rolled by and work continued taking precedence in Max's life. His job at Hickmans was finally picking up and his wage now surpassed his salary before the downturn. He decided that perhaps it was an appropriate moment to tackle Antonio about handing in his notice; to thank him for giving him the opportunity to rise from the gutter, as it were, but now with his finances on a more stable footing the time had come, he believed, to spend more quality time with his family. Max felt it wasn't an unreasonable request and he was sure Antonio, who was always addressing him as his friend, would understand.

"Max, old boy." Max hated it when Antonio started talking to him in that patronising manner. "How could we possibly manage without you? You know so much, too much some might say!"

Max felt uncomfortable – was he being threatened? He wasn't so naive as to believe that either Antonio or Marco weren't capable of making a person disappear off the face of the earth. In fact, it had even occurred to him that his predecessor – who it seemed, had disappeared apparently overnight – might have upset them in some way and had come to an untimely end.

"Look, Antonio, I'm grateful you've helped me through a difficult period, but if you remember, we did agree it was only temporary. If you like I could work until you find someone to replace me."

"Max, knowledge can be such a dangerous thing. I'm sorry, really I am, but I'm not willing to let you go just yet. Make the most of your good fortune, my friend, nothing lasts forever."

Max reluctantly dropped the subject for the time being, trusting that an opportunity would arise in the near future which would enable him to break from the perilous, self-inflicted situation in which he found himself.

One evening in November of '97, while Max was working alone on the computer in Heath Street, he inserted a new floppy disk and meticulously downloaded some of the information from the files. Removing the disk carefully, he stored it, with some satisfaction, in his briefcase – a guarantee, he hoped, for his and his family's future survival.

Arriving at the Heath Street office the following morning, Max was surprised to encounter a hubbub of activity taking place in the other rooms.

"Nothing for you to be concerned with, Max, old boy," Antonio reassured him, placing a hand on his shoulder. "Just moving things around for the sake of it; you might hear more noise than usual in the evenings. Best to keep your door shut, my friend, ok?"

Max made up his mind there and then: it was time he found out exactly what was going on behind those locked doors. An opportunity presented itself a few days later, when Antonio absentmindedly left a key ring containing three keys on his desk. Quickly, Max took impressions of each of them using the Blu-Tack from his desk drawer before Antonio returned, angry with himself for leaving them behind.

Later that evening, a commotion outside in the corridor forced Max to leave his desk. Stepping out into the dimly lit passageway, he was disturbed by the sight of Antonio trying to drag a screaming Candy back into the room next door. Realising that any intervention on his part would only add to the trauma taking place, Max turned and walked back into his office and carefully closed the door behind him. He was in torment. What sort of human being had he become? The old Max would not have hesitated to step in to help the distressed girl.

Several days later, he was preparing to make his weary way home when Candy appeared in the doorway.

"Max, I know you saw us the other night. Can I talk to you for a minute? I have no one else to turn to," Candy pleaded, removing her dark glasses and exposing a black eye.

"I'm on my way home, Candy. Can we talk tomorrow?" Max replied, trying to clear his desk quickly. He felt uneasy about getting involved in what he had perceived as a lover's tiff. Candy leaned in towards him across the desk – he could smell the alcohol on her breath.

"I found them; Antonio and one of those whores in the romper room. At it!"

Max looked puzzled. "Romper room?"

Candy smiled as she removed a long cigarette from its gold case. "That's what I call the room next door. You do know what's going on in there, Max, don't you?"

Max looked perplexed as he offered her a light for the cigarette, which lay contentedly between her red, pouting lips.

"Dear, innocent, lovely, Max," she cooed while she rounded his desk and sat seductively in front of him, before slowly crossing her long, shapely legs. "Haven't you seen the men coming and going recently? It's a knocking shop." She was slurring badly, Max wondered if it was a mix of drink and drugs. "Marco had to move his premises here temporarily, he got wind the cops were about to close him down."

Carefully, she stubbed out her cigarette and eased herself from the desk before throwing open her leather coat to reveal she was wearing nothing but white, lacy underwear. A heart-shaped tattoo on her inner thigh was the only blemish on her perfect, tanned skin. Max couldn't help but be aroused by this vision before him; after all, he was a normal red-blooded male.

Twisting him around in his chair to face her, she climbed onto his lap, gyrating enticingly. "I've always fancied you, you know," she revealed as she reached down and released his zip; slipping her hand through the opening, she began to fondle his manhood. Max was in turmoil. Oh, how it would be so easy to take this beautiful woman now across his desk; it would be most men's fantasy, but he knew he had to be strong or carry the guilt of betraying Josie for the rest of his life.

"Stop, Candy. Just stop, it's not going to happen," he said, reluctantly removing her hand from his trousers. "You're upset. Having sex with me will only make matters more complicated."

Furious at the rejection, she leapt to her feet, closing her coat, and yelled hysterically, "I'll tell the bastard you were the best fuck I've ever had, that you're more of a man than he is!" With that, she stormed out of the room without looking back.

Max didn't waste any time in collecting his things together. Letting himself out of his office, he swiftly made his way to the station. On the train home he decided to avoid any further confrontation, he would text Antonio he was unwell and wouldn't be in the next day, hoping that by Monday, Candy would have calmed down.

***

Saturday morning arrived and Max was settled down

in his favourite chair near the fire to read the paper. He had hardly slept the last couple of nights; his conscience in tormented overdrive. How could he have been so stupid to have found himself mixed up with Antonio? If only he could go back in time to that park bench and simply walk away. He even contemplated, in the early morning hours, packing everything up and going home with his family to Australia – but he knew it would be impossible to persuade Josie without coming clean about his shamed involvement with the Borelli family.

Unfolding the daily paper, his eye immediately fell on the lead story on the front page: 'Rumours Rife over Castle Street Stabbing', and instantly he was overcome with repulsion at its disclosure. The gruesome article went on to relate that the body of a blonde woman with multiple knife wounds, evidence of a horrifyingly violent attack, had been discovered in the early hours of Friday morning. The only distinguishing mark on the deceased was a heart-shaped tattoo on her right leg. He knew at once that the murder victim was Candy.

What the hell should he do now? It was too late to help the poor girl, but he had to do something. Why had Candy been killed? Had she carried out her threat and told Antonio she had sex with him? Was an enraged Antonio now out to kill him too? His imagination was running wild.

The obvious thing to do was to contact the police but, knowing how manipulative Antonio and Marco could be, could the police be trusted? Or did the Borelli family pay those in high places to turn a blind eye? If members of the force were on the pay roll, and the brothers wanted revenge, they might get him arrested on some drummed-up charge. What good would he be to his family then? No, he couldn't trust anyone.

Without much explanation to Josie, he left the cottage, clutching tightly the keys he had previously had cut. Arriving at his office in Heath Street, he checked out the area first to make sure the coast was clear before he let himself in. His instincts told him that if Antonio was the killer he had probably gone into hiding and would be well away from the area by now. He made himself a strong cup of coffee to settle his nerves before heading to the room next door.

Holding the keys in his trembling hand, he was relieved when his second attempt fitted perfectly. The door swung open into a small hallway, from which Max observed that the previously sizeable room had been divided into three distinct areas. Looking into the first one, he came upon an enormous bed draped with black silk sheets; large mirrors festooned the walls and ceiling, while a strong smell of perfume enveloped his nostrils. It certainly looked like his perception of a brothel. He pushed down the handle of the door opposite, but it was locked. Trying the other two keys in his hand, he found one that fitted.

The room beyond was crammed with technical equipment – a computer, cameras, and various monitoring screens. So, he thought to himself, they must have been filming the performances of the people in the bedrooms, for whatever perverted reasons. He reached into his pocket and retrieved the floppy disk, already holding incriminating evidence. With great speed, he inserted it into the slot in the computer and, without seeing exactly what it was copying, he let it do so until the disk was full.

Closing the door behind him, he once again thought of the vulnerable, beautiful Candy, who had been so full of life. Did she have a mother and father to grieve over her, he wondered, and if so, what had been the situation at home to have driven their daughter from their side, into the arms of such animals?

Later that night, Max rose from his warm place next to Josie and moved stealthily into his study, with the sole intention of exposing the contents of the disk. Immediately, he found himself sickened by the visions of both men and women taking part in various sexual acts on the screen. The final pictures, however, left him completely distraught – vile images of Candy lying in a pool of her own blood.

In his enraged state of mind, had Antonio been unaware that the camera was still running, recording him brandishing the knife with which he had eradicated her young life? Max was sure Antonio had been oblivious to this fact and would certainly be very keen to destroy this evidence when he eventually realised it existed; clear evidence, which had the power to send Antonio to prison for a very long time.

Without faltering, Max decided to make a second copy of the disk. He realised that if Antonio had no qualms about murdering Candy, then his life and possibly his family's lives were in grave danger. For some reason he still could not bring himself to go to the police, believing it was time he took control of his life; man up, and deal with Antonio himself.

It was also at this point that Max made the surprising decision to take a trip home. Once again, his actions forced him to lie to Josie. He told her he was sorry to leave her and the girls, but his trip was all about work and he had no choice in the matter. However, his actual plan was to speak in person to someone at the bank in Cairns, to make sure his accounts were in order, and afterwards visit Annie, to leave the second tape in her capable hands. It was fantastic seeing her warm, smiling face again, after such a prolonged lapse of time.

***

Back home in England, his life was much better than it had been for a long time. It helped that both Antonio and Marco had gone into hiding and were incommunicado. In the meantime, the Heath Street building had been emptied and boarded up, leaving no trace of it ever having been occupied. Naively, Max began to believe there was a definite possibility that this chapter of his life was over at last.

Christmas came and went, then at the beginning of February, unexpectedly, came a menacing call from Antonio that sent chills through Max's very soul.

"Max? Max, old boy, it's been a long time. How are you and your family, all well I hope?"

"Antonio ... what do you want?"

"What do I want? That's not much of a greeting, my friend. Thought it was time we had a little chat. By the way, have the police been in touch with you?"

"No, why should they have been?"

"I think you know, Max. I think you know more than is good for you, my friend. I warned you about going into the other offices, but you just wouldn't listen. We've seen you on video you see, entering one of the rooms."

Beads of sweat began to form on Max's brow as

his mind went into overdrive. "Yes, I was there, can't really deny it, can I? The door was open, I was looking for you."

"Oh, I see. Well I'm sure Marco will be comforted by your explanation, he's been a little ... let's say anxious, recently. He tried to persuade me you were a danger to the family, but I told him he needn't worry, I told him if we went down you'd be joining us and I know you would hate that Max. I know you would hate leaving your family."

Max realised Antonio had not mentioned Candy. Perhaps he had been wrong all along about the reason for her death; perhaps she had not told him they had sex. Perhaps it was simply a lover's quarrel, which went horribly wrong.

Max reached deep within himself and said with confidence, "Antonio, I've collected data that will send you away for a long time, but I won't use it as long as you leave me and my family alone." The long silence from Antonio brought Max further anguish. Had he gone too far?

"I think," Antonio began at last, "we should meet, soon, and Max, bring your data. I'd like to see it."

Max had felt a renewed strength at the end of the phone, but how would he feel when he actually came face to face with Antonio? To mask his potentially dangerous assignation, Max decided to book some time off from Hickmans to cover his absence – without telling Josie, so, as far as she was concerned, he would be going to work as usual.

They arranged to meet at the café at the end of Castle Street, the very street where the lifeless body of Candy had been discovered – although, as Max knew, not where she had been so brutally murdered.

He arrived early and seated himself at the table by the window, so he could see Antonio approaching. Next to him sat his briefcase, with his initials neatly embossed on the side – a present from his beloved wife. The floppy disk, clearly labelled '1 of 2', was within the leather container, ready to be offered up as the reason for Antonio not to hurt him or his family.

Gazing out from the window, Max's vision was slowly becoming impaired due to a dense fog now forming in the streets outside, bringing an eerie atmosphere to the scene, which in turn intensified the already tight feeling in the pit of his stomach.

Antonio was late.

After several mugs of tea, Max's nerves were definitely getting the better of him. Was Antonio playing games? Where the hell was he?

CHAPTER 3 – HOPES AND DREAMS

"Please come back to bed Josie, the rain won't stop just because you're watching it," Max mused, pulling back the covers, enticing his new wife to return to his side. Turning from the window, she looked at him and smiled before moving gracefully towards the bed and retaking her place next to him once more. Snuggling down contentedly, she could feel the heat radiating from his body, making her feel protected and cared for.

"I can't believe I'm finally Mrs. Josie Forrester. I do love you, you know."

"I should hope so, that wedding cost me a fortune!"

"What do you mean? Dad paid."

"He didn't buy my suit, it cost all of forty-five-pounds, do you know how many shifts at the pub I had to do to pay for it, my girl?" he teased, kissing her lips, before, not for the first time that morning, taking her in his arms and making love to her.

It was the summer of '81; their wedding had taken place in a rather antiquated London registry office, just weeks after their graduation, in the presence of Josie's family and their mutual university friends. They were now on honeymoon for four days in a Bournemouth hotel, not far from the beach.

"You know when we get back to the flat we will have to look for jobs, Josie. I know your parents have been really great but we do need to stand on our own two feet, my darling."

"You mean I'm not to be a lady of leisure? I thought you promised I'd want for nothing," she mocked, "or was that just a ploy to get me to go to bed with you?"

"It worked, didn't it?" He laughed.

***

Two months later, they had both found jobs in the City working as accountants. Although still renting a poky little one bed flat in London, they yearned for the peace and quiet of the countryside. Then, one evening, Josie arrived home laden with yet more details of properties given to her by over-enthusiastic estate agents.

"Max, Max please take a look, just for a minute, there must be one or two you'd like to see," she begged. Max sighed. They had been looking for months now; everything they had been interested in was well out of their price range.

"What about this one? It needs some work, but I'm sure dad would help in doing it up; you know how he loves DIY. Max, please just take a look."

Reluctantly, Max took the sheet from his wife's hand and studied the details closely. 'An easy commute into London, countryside views and two pubs', the estate agent's blurb pointed out.

"Ok, phone the estate agents and make an appointment to see it this weekend, but I'm not making any promises. Mind you, the two pubs might just swing it though." Josie threw her arms around her husband and kissed him hard.

***

From the moment they drove into Willow Green, Josie felt she had come home. The large, ancient village situated south of the Thames, oozed charm with its cobbled streets and quaint thatched-roofed dwellings encircling the village green.

Nestling comfortably at the end of a leafy lane was, as it turned out, the property of their dreams. Standing for the first time in front of Brook Cottage, their hearts pounded joyously. Before them, a small, flowered garden lined a winding path that led up to the entrance, adorned by a blood-red climbing rose; the old Victorian door seemed to beckon them in – bliss.

They soon settled down into the slower pace of village life but, unfortunately, there was still the little matter of work to pay for it all. Every morning they would leave at the same time to catch the six-thirty train to Embankment. Josie was usually home first, so she had no option but to prepare dinner, which involved opening a packet or taking something from the freezer, or, when she really couldn't be bothered, a phone call to the local Chinese or Indian to order a takeaway.

They both rolled into bed at night exhausted, but in the early morning light, well, things were different – Max was still the most sensual lover Josie had ever known. She couldn't imagine life not waking up with him, without the close intimacy they shared on those private, precious mornings together.

Then, unexpectedly, Josie found out she was pregnant. "Definitely not planned," she told the doctor's receptionist as she arrived at the surgery for her appointment, who in turn gave her a knowing smile. "My husband's excited though," Josie added nervously, before taking her seat in the crowded waiting room.

An hour later, her name was called. "Doctor Daniels will see you now, Mrs. Forrester. It's the second door on the left." Recognising Josie's anxious look, the receptionist added, "Don't worry, my dear, he won't bite."

Doctor Daniels was a man of about fifty, who, she had been told by the woman at the village post office, had worked and lived in and around Willow Green for most of his life. He looked up as Josie entered.

"Please take a seat, Mrs. Forrester. Haven't seen you here before, have I?"

"No, we only moved to the area last year."

"I see. Well, you'll be pleased to know the test has come back positive, so I'd better examine you."

Several minutes later, Josie left the surgery clutching an appointment card for her first scan. Although beginning to accept her pregnancy, uppermost in her mind was the worry about money and how were they going to pay the bills on just one salary, because Max had been very insistent that he did not want her to return to work. He had assured her they would manage – they had no choice. Just meant tightening their belts a bit; definitely no more takeaways, and holidays were certainly out of the question – for a while at least. Yes, she knew they would manage; no doubt about it. After all, they were both used to dealing with money, albeit other people's.

***

Waiting on her own outside the scan room, she wished Max was with her to share this special moment and to hold her hand. He had been most apologetic, of course, about being unable to go with her, but he had a meeting he couldn't get out of. All the same, she wished he were here.

On her arrival at the clinic, the nurse had asked her to make sure she drank lots of water and now her bladder was feeling most uncomfortable; she was desperate for a pee. Another expectant mother arrived and sat down opposite her.

"Hi, I'm Linda, any chance you need the ladies like I do?"

Josie looked over in her direction and grinned. "Yes, I hope I don't have to wait much longer. My name is Josie, by the way. How many weeks are you?"

"Sixteen, and you?"

"About the same."

"Well, Josie, we'll no doubt be seeing a lot of each other over the next few months. Look, I've got this craving for a cream cake, would you like to join me when we've finished here? There's a little tea room not far from the hospital, I've become a bit of a regular just recently. Would you be up for it?"

"Yes, sounds good," Josie replied, just as the nurse put her head around the door and indicated it was her turn.

***

The tearoom was indeed a pleasant place to while away a few hours. "So Linda, do you work?" asked Josie as she poured herself another cup of tea.

"Yes, I'm a hairdresser; I hope to have my own salon some day with the help of my ex-husband."

Josie looked surprised. "Ex-husband?"

Linda stroked her stomach. "Not officially ex, not

yet. Shaun left me for a slapper, some young thing about nineteen, before he knew I was pregnant."

"You don't seem too upset about it – I know I would be."

"To tell you the truth, he was a complete arse. It wasn't the first time I had caught him out, good luck to her I say, she'll need it."

***

Years went by and Josie and Max were still 'managing'. Their family had been completed sometime before with the arrival of a second daughter, Beth, a sister for Emma. With both girls now well established at the local primary school, Josie wondered if it was time to go back to work. The truth was, she was bored.

Yes, it was nice being able to take the girls to school and then always be there at the school gate to pick them up with all the other mothers. However, when she was home on her own, she missed the buzz her working life had brought her. She definitely wasn't the domestic type.

"Max," she began one day, "I've been thinking about going back to work. Would you have any objections?"

Unfortunately, Max felt quite indignant by her suggestion and immediately put his foot down. "The girls need you and your parents are too far away to help out, Josie." He pointed out. "If you need more money you know you only have to ask and anyway, I think things are picking up at work, I'm confident I'll get a promotion soon."

Famous last words – a deep recession hit the

country. Companies were going bust or laying off workers at an alarming rate. Surprisingly though, Max didn't seem too worried; life went on as usual, except for the mornings.

Now he would leave for work even before she awoke from her troubled sleep, that is, if he had come home at all. She was sick and tired of getting calls to say he was working late, or a meeting had overrun so he was staying in town. It had even crossed her mind he was seeing another woman. She shared these unbearable thoughts with Linda, when they met for coffee one morning.

"I'm sure you've nothing to worry about, sweetie. He's just working harder since this bloody recession. Hit my salon, you know. People stop having their hair done so often when money is tight. Had to let one of my stylists go last week, nice girl, but I go by the old saying 'last in, first out'."

Josie took a long sip of her coffee. "I hope you're right, Linda." She certainly hadn't stopped loving Max; she was just despairing to think the close relationship they had once shared together might be lost forever.

"Mind you, sweetie, now don't get upset at what I'm about to say but, well, when I first met you, even though you were pregnant I thought how smartly you always dressed. Just recently, well ..."

Josie looked down at her clothes. Linda was right. Her jogging bottoms, which she seemed to live in these days, even had a bleach mark she hadn't noticed before.

"How did I become such a slob? It's being in the house day after day. I've got to pull myself together; I don't want to lose Max. Can you help me to get back to the girl he fell in love with?"

"Ok, first of all, tomorrow I'll take you shopping, sweetie, and then I think it's time you had another talk with Max about getting a job, don't you?"

CHAPTER 4 – NEW BEGINNINGS

With her daughters both settled in grammar school, Josie believed Linda's advice was spot on; she should definitely tackle Max again about getting a job. She thought long and hard, and decided she did not want to go back to working as an accountant in the city and anyway, she had been away from that working environment so long, she would be out of touch with new practices. No, she needed a complete career change.

She decided to enquire at the nearest university about teacher training courses. With her enthusiasm heightened, she obtained all the information needed to put a good case to Max. At least being a teacher, like her father, would mean she was at home with the girls during the holidays and the training would only take a year because she already had a degree.

One evening, Josie made every effort to impress her husband: cooked him his favourite dinner of steak and chips, donned a sexy little black dress which showed off her ample cleavage (a purchase she had made while out shopping with Linda after a couple glasses of wine) and waited patiently for him to come through the door.

Late as usual, Max strolled in, threw down his briefcase haphazardly on the floor and commenced loosening his tie before slumping into the large leather chair closest to the roaring coal fire. Wearily, he closed his eyes as if to block out the world.

Carefully, Josie poured him a very large whiskey into an impressive cut glass goblet.

"I've cooked your favourite tonight, darling. Steak and chips," she revealed, encouraging him to leave his chair and join her at the table.

Reluctantly, he rose from the comfort of his seat and took his dutiful place opposite his wife. Only when he had finished the banquet she had set before him, and downed two large glasses of red wine, did Josie make her move.

"Max, please listen without interrupting me, as you usually do. Believe me, what I'm about to say is not a whim, I've been contemplating it for ages." She took a deep breath. "I'd like to go back to work. I know you were against it a little while ago, but the girls are older now and, quite frankly, they hate it when I meet them out of school and keep telling me they would rather walk with their friends. I don't want to return to the rat race of London – couldn't stand the commute – but I would like to train as a teacher, then at least I would be around in the school holidays. Well, what do you say?"

She came to the end of her prepared speech and looked at Max waiting for a response, waiting for her ideas to be dismissed by her husband. However, all he said, in a very exhausted voice, was, "Do as you like, darling, whatever makes you happy. I'm going to bed; it's been a long day." With that, he got up, left the room and did not speak about it again.

***

"I'm so pleased he didn't put up a fight. Told you that dress would work! Good for you, sweetie. How about coming out for a drink to celebrate?" Linda enthused on the other end of the phone.

"Sounds like a good idea, but I promised Beth I would help her with a history project. Another time, perhaps. Anyway, I thought you had a date with that bank manager."

"He cancelled on me. His loss!"

***

Josie was a keen learner, she enjoyed the thrill of getting into a new routine, juggling her coursework and family life; she felt she had found herself once more. No longer just a mum or a wife, she was now Josie Forrester, student teacher. The months flew by and before she knew it, she had qualified with top grades, ready and eager to inspire the future generation.

Looking through the job vacancy page in their local paper one Wednesday, Josie's eyes were immediately drawn to an advertisement for a maths teacher at her daughters' school.

"Emma, Beth, you didn't tell me there was a job going at your school, who's leaving?" Josie asked, ringing the advert with a red pen.

Emma looked at her sister, seemingly electing who should answer. "Mrs. Thornton's retiring. My friend Abigail's in her class and apparently she had a complete breakdown in front of them, just because someone wrote 'Mrs. Thornton smells' on her blackboard and wouldn't own up. She kept the entire class in after school, insisting their parents collected them so she could tell them what horrible children they are."

"I see, I'm sure that's not the only reason she decided to retire. Anyhow, I think I'll apply for the position."

Together they chorused, "No, mum, please no, it would be so embarrassing if you worked at our school."

"Sorry girls, to be honest it's the only one in the paper this week, I've got to at least try. Anyway I might not get an interview, let alone the job." Emma and Beth crossed their fingers tightly behind their backs, praying she wouldn't.

Josie did get a reply to her application and sometime later attended a very formal interview at the school. She felt slightly intimidated, facing not only the Headmistress, but also the board of governors, who bombarded her with question after question. Nevertheless, to the dismay of Emma and Beth, who consequently ran around the cottage screaming that their lives had ended, Josie started working at Felix Grammar School for Girls in September '97, and she loved every minute.

Weekends were now taken over with cleaning, shopping, and preparing lessons for the following week. Josie was in her element – she just wished Max would do more to help her around the house. Instead, every Saturday morning he would just sit reading the paper from start to finish.

Except for one particular Saturday in November, when Max seemed more distant than usual and after thoroughly scanning the lead story 'Rumours Rife over Castle Street Stabbing', he immediately folded the paper and informed her he was going out and would not be back until dinner.

Then, three weeks before Christmas, without

warning Max announced he was off on a whirlwind trip to Cairns in Australia for his company Hickmans. "I'm sorry Josie, I know I've always planned to take you to my home one day, but this is business, Mr. Forbes insists I go, I really can't get out of it."

"Hasn't he heard of email or post? What could be so important that you have to go half way around the world?" She cried.

Max looked at her and then sighed. "We have this important client who's in Cairns at the moment trying to secure a deal and he wants some sensitive documentation brought back here. Apparently he doesn't trust modern technology."

She helped him pack a small bag and kissed him goodbye at the station, craving a passionate embrace from the man she loved, but it was not to be.

Max was only away for five days but to Josie it seemed a lifetime. Surprisingly, he appeared to be in a better mood, once he had overcome his jet lag, as if a huge weight had been lifted from his shoulders. He even came up behind her in the kitchen one evening, when the girls were firmly tucked up in bed, and put his arms around her, caressing her breasts while nibbling her neck affectionately.

Eventually their passion took them to the privacy of their bedroom where they lay together in a fiery fervour, delighting in each other's pleasure with such youthful enthusiasm that, for a moment in time, no one else in the world mattered.

***

They all had a wonderful Christmas. Josie's parents spent Christmas and Boxing Day at their cottage. Her mother hovered over Josie as she prepared the turkey, giving advice, and – although well meant – it made Josie nervous and more than a little tetchy. She was determined they would have a harmonious time, so managed to smile through gritted teeth.

"How long has the bird been in, Josie dear? Only, too long and it'll dry out you know. Do you think there are enough potatoes? You know your father loves his roast potatoes, and are you making your own gravy or are you using that packet stuff?"

"Mum, I have cooked Christmas dinner before. How about making the custard for the Christmas pudding? No one makes custard like you." Josie always seemed to know the right thing to say to her mum.

At the end of the two days, everyone said how much they had enjoyed the festivities. The girls got the cassette players they had wanted and Josie gave Max the leather jacket he had been drooling over in her clothes catalogue. Max's present to Josie, however, astounded her. He usually bought her a jumper or a handbag, which she always said she loved, but added: did he have the receipt? Not this Christmas.

When they woke on Christmas morning to the screams of the girls opening their presents, Max rolled over to Josie and presented her with a small box wrapped in shiny gold paper and topped with an elaborate bow.

"Open it then," Max insisted, eager to see his wife's face. Carefully, she peeled back the polished paper and opened the small red box within. The card read, 'To my darling wife, thank you for marrying me, Max xxx'. Inside was a large diamond ring, which shone so brightly it cast dancing lights around their bedroom.

"Max, Max how could you afford...?" Josie began, but Max took her in his arms and kissed her ardently on her lips as if to reassure her she needn't worry about the cost – he loved her and would always love her.

The New Year began with a heavy fall of snow bringing transport to a halt. Schools and businesses were temporarily closed. The girls were delighted to have a few extra days of holiday, which they spent with their dad sledging on the Downs behind their cottage. Once the snow stopped falling and the roads turned to a horrible brown slush, life gradually got back to normal.

Soon, before they knew it, it was the first Tuesday in February, a day embedded in Josie's heart; the day her whole world came crashing down. It started normally, Max rushing off early to catch the train and almost forgetting his sandwiches, and the girls, as usual, not wanting to rise from their warm beds, shouting at each other as they vied for the only bathroom in the cottage.

At last, peace and quiet. Josie, for once, did not have to be in school until later. She started clearing away the breakfast things then switched on the kettle for a much needed cup of tea, ahead of marking Year 5's homework. Just before eleven-thirty, the doorbell rang. Josie sighed. What now? Would she ever get a moment to herself? Opening the door, she was taken aback to set eyes on two police officers standing on her doorstep.

"Mrs. Forrester, we need to speak to you. Can we come in please?" the female police officer requested gently.

"Yes of course, I'm sorry the cottage is in a bit of a mess; not had a chance to tidy yet. Can I get you both a cup of tea?"

"No thank you, Mrs. Forrester." The officers both looked at her gravely. "I'm so sorry, Mrs. Forrester, but we've reason to believe your husband has been involved in a traffic accident."

"What are you saying? How badly is he hurt? Which hospital have they taken him to? I must go and see him. I'll find my bag." She started rummaging wildly about her. "Now where the hell did I put my bag?"

"Mrs. Forrester, I'm so sorry, but the man we believe is your husband died at the scene."

"No, no you must have got that wrong; he left for work this morning. I'll phone his office, he's there, I know he is."

The following few minutes passed in a blur. She knew there were people speaking but she seemed to be in a trance and those around her appeared to move in slow motion.

Reaching down into a plastic bag, the male police officer produced Max's blood splattered coat, together with his leather briefcase with his initials clearly marked.

"These items were recovered with the body, Mrs. Forrester. We discovered Mr. Forrester's name and address on some letters in the case. Do you recognise them?"

Josie clasped the bag in her hand. "Yes ... yes, they're my husband's. I bought this bag for him on his last birthday."

So, there was no mistake. Tears welled up in her

eyes and began their shattered descent down her now ashen face and then this loud, uncontrollable wail came from deep within her soul. Doctor Daniels arrived and gave her something to help her sleep, but that was the last thing she wanted to do. She wanted to run; she wanted to find him, to hold him one last time – Max, the love of her life.

CHAPTER 5 - DARK SHADOWS

David looked at his daughter's bowed head with tears forming in his eyes. Standing in the small village church on that cold February morning he wished, oh how he wished, he could ease her pain. If he had only been there on that dreadful morning to push Max out of the way of that evil coward who had left his daughter and grandchildren in such despair.

He had been the one the police asked to identify Max's body. It was not the first time he had set eyes on a corpse, but when it is a member of your own family, someone you had shared so many memories with, well, it's near impossible to eradicate the vision of the destroyed human being that was once your son-in-law.

Looking down at the remains laying on the cold slab, David remembered being deeply disturbed at the way his skull had been crushed – like an annihilated watermelon after falling from a great height. Thank god Josie had been spared this image of the man she loved.

Even though the body was so obviously damaged, the police seemed quite satisfied with David's identification and even apologised to him for putting him through such a traumatic ordeal.

***

Josie picked up a handful of soil and tossed it over

Max's coffin. At length, the gathering left the graveside and both girls put their arms around their mother. Heads bowed, they sobbed quietly into sodden handkerchiefs. Josie was unaware of anyone else around her up until this point; her despair had totally overtaken her body and her mind. However, as her children guided her towards the awaiting funeral car, she could not help but notice two men, unknown to Josie, standing a short distance away. When they realised she had seen them they nodded their heads towards her, before turning and heading back to their waiting limousine.

The sombre cavalcade headed off to the White Horse Hotel, where Josie's parents had arranged a small buffet tea for the fifty or so mourners. Several people from the village had gathered to show their respect and immediately approached her to say how sorry they were, what a nice man he was, and if she ever needed anything, she only had to ask.

A tall, well-groomed man in a rather expensive grey pinstriped suit made his way purposefully towards her and took her hand in his. "I'm so sorry to meet you under these circumstances, Mrs. Forrester. I'm Mr. Forbes, I was Max's boss. He was such a dedicated member of staff."

Josie stared directly into the eyes of the infamous Mr. Forbes, who, she believed, was the main reason her husband had been compelled to work to the point of exhaustion.

Biting her tongue, lest she say anything untoward, Josie spoke warily, "Thank you for coming, Mr. Forbes. Max told me so much about you. Would you like a drink?"

"Yes, thank you, just a small one. I have to get

back to work." Josie handed him a glass of sherry, from which Mr. Forbes took a long sip before continuing. "Do the police have any more leads as to who the driver was?"

Josie took a deep breath; she really didn't want to talk about this now, not at Max's funeral, especially with the man she felt had been the cause of so much tension in her relationship with her husband. "'Err, no, but they tell me they will leave no stone unturned, as it were. Would you please excuse me, Mr. Forbes, I must talk to the vicar before he leaves."

"Yes, of course, I understand." He put down his glass but persisted in talking to Josie as she attempted to walk away. "Such a stickler for time: arrived at nine and always had his coat on by five-thirty. Was Max on a shopping trip, by the way?" Mr. Forbes enquired.

"Sorry?" Josie turned back at once to face him.

"I asked if Max was on a shopping trip. After all, he had booked a few days off. Would have thought coming back up to London was the last thing he would want to do."

It was at this point that a wave of nausea enveloped her and the room started to spin. She emitted a muffled gasp before plummeting to the floor. Her mother and Linda rushed to her aid and gently led her away to a small room to lie down.

Was she hearing things? Max always left the office on time. Had booked some time off?

As June left the room, Josie spoke quietly to Linda, "I need to talk to you. Will you come to the cottage when this is all over?"

"Of course, sweetie. I'll stay the night if you want me to."

***

The cottage seemed colder than usual. "Soon have the fire going," David remarked as he started to scrunch the very newspaper that had carried the story of Max's death.

Josie had no interest in reading any newspapers, especially one where a picture of a smiling Max looked back at her. The article, which had been written by a highly respected reporter, mentioned the fact that this was the second death in Castle Street in recent months and that New Scotland Yard detectives were at the crime scene, led by Chief Inspector Wainwright.

David meticulously festooned the discarded paper with the kindling Max had chopped only a few weeks before. The crackling fire rapidly threw invisible columns of roaring heat up into the room.

"We'll take the girls back with us, if you like, give you time to rest properly." June spoke quietly, whilst giving Beth a much needed cuddle.

"Yes, thanks mum. Linda's staying with me tonight."

Soon after David and June had left with the girls, Linda and Josie settled down in front of the fire with large mugs of hot Ovaltine. Pulling a blue throw closely around her shivering body, Josie broke the silence.

"Do you remember the conversation we had when I thought Max was cheating on me? Well, today I learned that he probably was, and the man I thought I knew had been leading a double life." Josie related Mr. Forbes chilling words. Linda, for once, was speechless. It certainly seemed, with this evidence, that Max was not the perfect husband she had always thought he was.

Why was he in London if he was not working? Did he, in fact, have a mistress stowed away somewhere in the area around Castle Street? If a mistress did exist, did she know what had happened to him? Was she with him when he had the accident? There were so many unanswered questions.

Later that night in their bed, like all the nights since Max's death, she sobbed uncontrollably into her tear-stained pillow, crying for the man she loved, though now she found herself in deep turmoil – had he, in fact, been in love with her?

The next day, the ringing tones of the phone echoed through the cottage. "Hello, hello." Click. No one answered, not even heavy breathing. Josie rolled over in bed and looked at the clock – nine-fifteen on a Saturday morning. She looked up as Linda's head appeared around the door.

"Are you decent? Thought you might need a cuppa." Handing her a much-welcomed cup of tea, Linda posed the question, "How did you sleep?"

"Not very well, must get up though, I need to fetch the girls. Will you come with me?"

"Of course, I'll stay with you as long as you want me to, ok?"

Josie smiled. "Thanks, what would I do without you?"

Just as they were leaving the house, the irritating sound of the phone rang out again. "Hello, hello, who is this?" Josie's voice was beginning to show the strain of the last few weeks.

"Kids I expect, sweetie, not worth getting stressed over. We have a lot of trouble with them at the salon."

Arriving at David and June's house, they were greeted warmly by Emma and Beth.

"Do you want to stay for lunch? It's not much,

just cold meat and salad." June pointed out, almost apologetically.

"That would be great mum, really." Josie realised there probably wasn't anything to eat at the cottage anyway; food shopping was the last thing on her mind.

In the kitchen, the place where most of her intimate conversations had taken place with her mother, she confided in both her parents her uncertainties about Max. Tears appeared in June's eyes and David thumped the worktop in anguish. They both put their arms around their beloved daughter and David kissed her cheek tenderly. "I don't want the girls to know, they thought their dad was wonderful and that's how I want them to remember him."

They drove back up to the cottage later that afternoon and walked along the winding path to the front door – to the opened front door!

"Anyone there?" Josie called out, her voice shaking with the prospect of someone lying in wait. She pushed the door carefully, revealing the darkened hall. "Emma, run next door with Beth and tell Mrs. Woods to phone the police – go now! Go quickly, darling, please."

"I think we should wait for them to arrive, Josie," whispered Linda. Too late, Josie was already in, but not before picking up the large, smooth grey stone that lay adjacent to the doormat, which confidently bore the words WELCOME.

Switching on the hall light, they moved cautiously from room to room. No sign of anyone, and nothing seemed to have been disturbed either. Linda smelt the air; a distinct whiff of a man's aftershave enveloped her – Brut, she had no doubt about it.

Reaching Max's office, Josie hesitated; she hadn't felt able to enter this area, Max's domain, since his death. The door was ajar. Stepping into the study, the sight that met their eyes was baffling. Nothing else in the cottage had been touched, but this room seemed like a bulldozer had trawled through it. The sound of police sirens and the pulsating blue lights brought them only a little comfort. What had the intruder been looking for, and why her house?

CHAPTER 6 – FEMALE DETECTIVES

The police said they were mystified as to the reason for the break in, especially as Josie's diamond ring was still sitting majestically in its box on the table next to her bed. The only obvious item missing was the computer. It hadn't been a state-of-the-art computer; in fact, it was large and the monitor cumbersome. Max had been moaning for ages he needed a new one, something a bit higher tech and of modern appearance, he had implored – now he would never get his wish.

There was so much paper strewn about the place that at first glance, Josie was unable to tell if anything else had been stolen. As far as she knew, most of the documents in the study related to the household bills or personal matters, certainly Max never kept anything work related around the house.

A week later, the police finally gave her permission to tidy the room. This is what she had been waiting for: time to sort out Max's paperwork, perhaps now she would find something to help her understand her husband's behaviour. It could be anything at all; photos, hotel bills, or such like. Max had always kept meticulous records and, even though they were now spread about in all directions, it was relatively easy to put the puzzle back together again.

However, she found nothing, nothing at all to suggest an affair – had Max been extra careful not to bring any evidence home? Then she came across an address in London written on a scrappy piece of paper tossed carelessly in the waste paper bin. She phoned Linda, who came immediately.

"I've looked at a London map and the address is very near to where Max was killed. It could mean anything, but perhaps he was going there that day. I can't just sit doing nothing, I've got to go and see, Linda," Josie emphasised defiantly.

"Yes of course, I'll go with you." Linda was worried her friend might unearth her worst nightmare – the confirmation that her precious Max had a mistress tucked away somewhere.

***

Although it was Sunday, the painfully slow train into town was almost full to bursting; perhaps some people were treating themselves to a show or a shopping trip ... whatever the reason for their journey, it could not possibly be the same as two amateur, would-be detectives, trying to unravel the trail of a potentially deceitful husband.

Eventually reaching their destination, they alighted from the carriage and, after a brisk walk, came across a sign mounted high on a brick wall confirming they were at the corner of Heath Street. Not the sort of place Josie had envisaged at all.

The narrow road that stretched out in front of them looked gloomy and the buildings that straddled the ancient path definitely upheld this feeling of neglect. They perceived that several windows had been boarded up, depriving the inner core of any possible sunlight. It seemed the last place you would imagine anyone, let alone Max, renting for a so-called 'love nest'.

"Here it is, numbers nineteen to twenty-five," Josie declared, checking the piece of paper she had been clutching firmly in her hand. They both looked up forlornly at the towering, bleak building. Reaching into her handbag, she retrieved a small torch she always kept for those just-in-case moments and this was definitely one of them. "Come on then, Linda," she urged, not wanting to waste any more valuable time.

Cautiously, they pushed the unlocked metal gate, whose hinges seemed to scream with protest at their disturbance, before starting the steady climb up the steep stone steps that rose up forebodingly in front of them – first floor, second floor.

"This is it," Josie pointed out as she arrived at the dark green door, the entrance to number twenty-three. Unfortunately, it was shut fast. A warning notice securely attached to it read: 'INTRUDERS WILL BE PROSECUTED KEEP OUT!'

"Oh my god, and after all those steps too," groaned Linda.

"But why would Max have this address? It doesn't make any sense." Josie walked along the corridor knocking on other doors to see if anyone was about, but to no avail. She felt frustrated. She had strongly believed they were going to resolve some of her questions here, but no, it seemed it was not to be. "Look Linda, we must be near where Max was knocked down."

"Yes, of course sweetie. Do you want to go and find the road?"

"Well, as we're here, you never know, perhaps it will give us some answers."

They descended the steps more rapidly than they

had climbed them; this was certainly not the place for a romantic dalliance. Turning the corner, Josie suddenly pulled Linda into an alleyway. "Look Linda, that man. I'm sure he was one of the men I saw at Max's funeral."

Linda looked towards a rather handsome, swarthy looking male in a long trench coat, who was striding out purposely towards the train station. "Are you sure it's one of them? You were pretty upset at the time."

"As sure as I can be. I wonder who he is, and what he's doing around here." With mounting curiosity, they watched the stranger from their hiding place in the alleyway as he rapidly disappeared into the station. Was it more than a coincidence he happened to be hanging around the exact place where Max had been killed?

Two streets later and there they were, facing Castle Street. Linda took hold of Josie's hand for comfort. A fading police notice, now barely attached to a lamppost, was asking for any eyewitnesses to a serious accident.

"Terrible bloody business," a croaky voice behind them announced, making them both jump.

"Did you see what happened?" Josie asked, spinning around and coming face to face with a scruffy looking vagrant.

"Saw the lorry, giant of a thing rumbling down the road going much too fast if you ask me, especially in that fog. Could hardly see your hand in front of your face that day, poor bloke wouldn't have stood a bloody chance when the lorry mounted the pavement. Seen the same lorry coming and going around here for years making deliveries, whoever was driving should have known better than to try and drive down this street, it's a well-known fact there's a size limit. Perhaps it was a different delivery driver. Foreigner, I reckon, yes, must have been a bloody foreigner," he was still mumbling as he turned and wandered away.

"That's it, that's why they can't find him, he must have been a foreign lorry driver. He could be anywhere in Europe by now," Josie speculated painfully. Linda squeezed her hand.

While she took one more look at the place where part of her life had ended so dramatically, large drops of rain began to fall, quickly saturating the ground around them. Josie's eyes looked skywards; were they tears from heaven, she pondered. Under her breath, she said a final goodbye to her husband and lover, then turned and, still holding Linda's hand, walked away.

The train journey home was, thankfully, much less crowded. "I'm going to the police station when we get back to talk to our family liaison officer, WPC Brown; she said I could speak to her any time. I realise we didn't really find out much today, but I think I should tell the police about Heath Street."

"Yes, well it can't hurt, can it? Anyway, if they think it's a possible lead, they might be able to gain entrance to number twenty-three by getting a court order or something."

Arriving back at Willow Green, they immediately set out towards the police station. The station sergeant explained if they wanted to talk to WPC Brown, they would have to wait in reception because she was in a meeting.

They sat twiddling their thumbs, until half an hour later the WPC appeared. "Hello Josie, and Linda, isn't it? Please, come this way."

She led them into her small office, housing a table and four rather uncomfortable metal chairs. Josie soon revealed everything to the young WPC, from the lie that was her marriage and concluding with their visit to Heath Street.

WPC Brown tapped her pencil and sat back in her chair. "Would you have any objections if I related some of this story to my chief inspector? I think he might find this intriguing." Was it the possibility that Max had been having an affair that interested her, thought Josie, or the address in Heath Street? Anyway, she agreed to the WPC passing on the information, if it would help with their enquiries – the more people on the case the better.

The chief inspector was indeed fascinated by Josie's story and even sent a CID team around to number twenty-three. However, the following evening, he phoned to inform her that they had not found any evidence that Max had been in the building. Therefore, frustratingly, she was no further forward in unravelling the mystery of why Max was in Castle Street.

Several weeks later, a police car drew up outside Josie's cottage, with the news that a Polish lorry driver had been caught and charged with Max's manslaughter. Apparently, he had been stopped at Dover for a routine check and was found to be carrying illegal immigrants.

After further police investigations, it was established that the Polish driver's regular route went through that area of London and he had actually been in the vicinity at the time when Max had been killed. Under interrogation, he had broken down and confessed to causing Max's death. The question was:

why was he driving on an unsuitable road when he was obviously familiar with the area? His answer was simple: He told the police that the road he usually took had been closed off and he had been diverted through Castle Street. Unfortunately for the driver, the police did not believe his story, mainly because they could find no evidence to support his claim. The arrest of the man brought little comfort to Josie, Max was still dead, nothing was ever going to bring him back, but perhaps now the family could move forward with their lives.

CHAPTER 7 – VALLEY VIEW

Unpacking the heavily loaded car in front of the imposing stone-built bungalow, Josie looked around her at the rolling green countryside before them. She never got tired of that view, the ever-changing valley that stretched on forever. She and Max had brought the girls down every year since they were little; watching them as they ran barefoot through the long grass, squealing with delight at the sight of colourful butterflies floating on the cool breeze. Now she was here again, with Emma and Beth but no Max. Instead, Linda and her son Patrick had joined them for a much-needed break.

"You finally made it, all of you," June cried, greeting them with much joy and relief. David and June had arrived a week earlier to open up the place and give it a good airing. They always made at least two journeys each year to their 'Devon estate', as they liked to call it. First, just before Easter, to make sure everything was fine and dandy for the summer holidaymakers and then again in late October, to close everything up for the winter.

They employed a letting agency to run the business side, but liked to keep a close eye on the operation themselves as well. Their intention had been to make the bungalow their retirement home, but now ... well, understandably, their plans were on hold for the near future.

"What an absolutely lovely place you have here,"

Linda remarked honestly, whilst taking in the idyllic vista around her, "and no neighbours to annoy, how glorious!"

"Of course, this is your first visit to Valley View, isn't it? Come, I'll give you a guided tour." David was always pleased to show people his pride and joy, which he had lovingly renovated over many years.

The heavy front door opened into a long, straight, narrow hall lined with inviting doors on both sides. While Josie and the girls followed her mother to the generous kitchen and dining room, which ran the whole length of the back of the bungalow, David showed Linda and Patrick into the lounge.

Light flooded into the large, but cosy, room, dominated by a huge bay window, taking full advantage of those awe-inspiring views.

"This is very impressive. I love the fire place, is it made out of local stone?" David delighted with her reaction, smiled and nodded while Linda continued to enthuse. "I could sit looking out of this bay window all day, I'd never get any work done; it's all wonderful, you're very lucky."

"Yes, we love it here. Shall we go and find the others? No doubt June will have made a pot of tea by now."

Joining Josie and her mother in the kitchen, David unlocked the French doors that opened up into a modest, fully stocked, walled garden. During the summer months, colourful perennials intermingled with well-kept shrubs and fragrant rose bushes. Now, the once-striking, dying heads of daffodils were being replaced by large red tulips, which were forcing their way proudly up into the spring sunshine, providing a tranquil place to sit on those precious sunny days.

"Close the door, David," moaned June, "there's a draught. How about showing Linda and Patrick where they're going to sleep?" Moving from the kitchen back into the corridor, David pointed to the doors to the left of the hallway.

"Those are the bedrooms. There are three altogether, we thought you and Josie could share this one." David opened the second door to expose a rather quaint room; two single beds, covered in green candlewick bedspreads, were the centrepiece. A large wardrobe, that had obviously seen better days, stood tall next to an almost matching chest of drawers. Vivid floral wallpaper decorated the four walls, making the room feel smaller than it actually was.

"Wow!" Linda exclaimed, glancing at Josie as she realised this was probably the room she and Max usually shared. "This looks fine, thank you."

"We thought Patrick could use the put up in the lounge, if that's alright with you?" June commented, suddenly appearing around the door.

Linda looked at her son as a huge grin began to cover his face. "I think that's a yes, June."

"Thanks mum," exclaimed Patrick. Of course, the young man was especially delighted as not only would he be the last to go to bed, but also it was the only room with a television, albeit an antiquated one.

After a satisfying dinner, the women remained in the kitchen whilst David joined the children for a game of cards in the front room.

"Has your father spoken to you about ... about what we found when we first arrived?" June began.

"When you arrived? No, he hasn't," returned Josie, intrigued.

June lowered her voice so the children couldn't

hear her. "Well, it looked like someone had been living here. It wasn't in a bad state, you understand, but definitely things had been disturbed; tins of food we left last September have disappeared together with some of your father's clothes." Josie and Linda put down their tea towels and listened intently. "We spoke to the letting agents and they admitted they hadn't been up here since February. February, I ask you! With all the money they charge, anything could have happened to the place."

"Your dad wasn't very happy, I can tell you. The strange thing is, the garden seems to have been tidied and the gate leading out to the woods at the back repaired. Your dad said it was one of the jobs he was going to deal with this holiday. We have reported it to the police, of course. They think whoever it was must be long gone by now."

"I certainly hope so," said Linda, trying to stop the tremble in her voice.

"Well, as long as they've gone and aren't lurking in the woods," Josie added, the disquieting words erupting from her mouth before she could stop herself.

The thought of someone lurking in the woods had not dawned on June, but now it was at the forefront of her mind, causing her slight panic. "We must make sure all the windows and doors are always tightly closed and the children, we must keep them within our sight when we're outside."

After kissing the excited girls goodnight, Josie snuggled down under the sheets and blankets. "Linda, what sort of person would be desperate enough to break into someone's house and live there without any consideration to the owners?"

"A selfish arse who believes society owes them, I should think. Don't worry too much about it sweetie, as the police said, they must be long gone by now. I mean, you hear about squatters all the time; at least they've left without causing any mess." Linda yawned and pulled the covers closer. "Nighty, night."

Josie shivered as she contemplated the realisation that her elderly parents could have arrived whilst the trespasser, or trespassers, were still there, sitting boldly in her dad's clothes whilst eating from the tins her parents had purchased at the small village shop just two miles down the road.

Perhaps, in their twisted minds, they had believed that working in the garden and repairing the gate was payment enough for their bed and board. Her mother hadn't mentioned how they had managed to break in. Through a window, would have meant there would have been broken glass everywhere. Even if they had cleared it up, would they not have needed a new pane to replace it? Josie drifted off to sleep with a head full of rational and irrational ideas circling apprehensively around it.

***

The week that followed was, the grown-ups decided, one for the kids. On Tuesday, they drove to Bideford in order to take a boat trip to Lundy, something they had done many times as a family before. Walking along the side of the road, taking them down to the boats' moorings, the image of Max holding her hand kept popping into Josie's head. She couldn't help it; he had always loved the coast, loved the sounds and smell of the sea. Boarding the rocking craft, Josie missed the strong arms that had always been there to help her as she wobbled, unsure of her footing, into the swaying vessel.

Several miles out, poor Linda found she definitely did not have sea legs and spent the time with her head over the ship's side, hurling into the swell below – she was more than relieved when they reached dry land again.

The next day, Linda began to feel a lot better and insisted she was up for the family's annual scenic cycle ride through Exmoor. It was only when they came to get the bikes out of the shed in the garden, they realised one was missing. The one Max usually rode.

"Bastards, they've taken the one with the torn seat. Bastards."

"Dad, the children!" Josie was alarmed at the venom in her dad's usually calm demeanour.

Emma put her arm lovingly around her granddad. Both she and Beth were still oblivious to the fact her grandparents had had an intruder. "It's ok, granddad, there's still enough bikes for all of us who want to use them. I expect it was a gypsy who wanted it to sell, not that they would get much for it as it rattled like an old bag of bones." Darling Emma always knew how to bring a smile to her granddad's face.

The days were bad enough for Josie, being full of memories of her life with Max, but the nights were even worse. During the sleepless quiet hours of darkness, Josie's mind went into overdrive. She remembered how she and Max would push the single metal beds together while trying to avoid the clanking noise the two old bedsteads inevitably made, as they slid with some difficulty across the patterned carpet.

Remembered how, amid the shadows of the night, they had laid there like forbidden teenage lovers, with their parents in the next room. Remembered how his hands had followed the contours of her yielding body as they caressed her intimate areas – enjoying the soft cries that came quietly from them both as they wrapped themselves in the warmth of their love making. Oh, how she missed that.

All too soon, the week came to an end. As they waved goodbye from the car window and started in a downward direction towards the steep spiral track, heavily framed by soaring hedgerows, Josie could not help but wonder if the unwanted trespassers were still lurking somewhere, waiting for everyone to leave, so they could resume their occupancy of their adopted dwelling.

CHAPTER 8 – A FACE FROM THE PAST

Waiting in Mr. Smyth's dingy office almost a month later, Josie shuffled uneasily in her seat. Mr. Smyth was her solicitor, who had summoned her to go over her financial situation following the sudden appearance of Max's will, which, unbeknownst to Josie, had been sitting in a bank in Cairns. Why Max had felt the need to make a will and leave it in an Australian bank without telling her, Josie had no idea; after all, they had very little spare money to save so working out their assets should be, she believed, a reasonably straightforward task.

Sitting opposite her in a large, imposing green leather chair, the weasel-like eyes of Mr. Smyth focused on Josie through round, metal-framed glasses. Clearing his throat, he began to read from the document he was clutching in his gnarled hands.

"Well, Mrs. Forrester, as expected, Max has left all his worldly goods to you, with a couple of provisos. He has set up trust funds for your daughters, which they will be able to access when they reach twenty-one."

Josie was not only astonished, but also intrigued at this latest disclosure, so much so she leant forward in her chair not wanting to miss any of the words he was uttering. "I see," she said, nodding in response.

"Yes, the money has been put into Australian funds; looks as if they were only set up at the end of last year."

Last year, when Max said he was on a trip for Hickmans; was she to understand he was actually sorting out his finances instead?

"Mr. Smyth, can you tell me the date on the will?" Josie enquired, believing she already knew the answer to her question.

"Twenty-ninth of November, 1997," her solicitor read from the top of the document.

Why, thought Josie, why had Max felt the need to write a will then? After all, they had talked about writing their wills together on several occasions, but the idea had, if she was truthful, always made them both feel a bit uncomfortable – as if doing so was putting a nail in their coffins.

"As for the money he has left you, well the mortgage has now been paid off, as I am sure you already know, with the insurance attached to your payments."

"Yes, I had a letter yesterday," Josie replied, recalling the neatly addressed envelope containing further confirmation of her widowed status.

Mr. Smyth continued with little emotion in his voice. "Apart from your joint bank accounts there is also another fund account in Australia which was opened in both your names, but obviously since Max's death it passes solely to you." He handed Josie a sheet of paper with account numbers for the First National in Cairns. "They wouldn't give me much information, I'm afraid. They are waiting to hear from you in person."

"Thank you, Mr. Smyth," Josie said, genuinely expressing her gratitude for the work he had put in.

"Are there any questions you would like to ask me?" he queried.

She deliberated her answer before replying. "None that I can think of at the moment, but if I do, I will certainly be in touch with you again."

Rising with some difficulty from his chair, Mr. Smyth stretched out his slender arm. Josie responded by extending hers, shaking the little man's hand. She wondered if there were any more surprises in store for her.

Back in the comforting walls of her cottage once more, she didn't give herself much time to catch her breath before dialling the number for the First National Bank in Cairns. Of course, in her desperate state to speak to someone, she forgot there was a time difference and only got an answer machine. Damn. Glancing at her watch, she calculated she needed to phone Australia about ten o'clock in the evening. It was an anxious wait until she dialled again.

"Hello, my name's Josie Forrester, I'm calling from England about my late husband's accounts."

"Just one moment, I'll put you through to one of our managers." The Australian voice at the end of the phone sounded very matter of fact.

"Mrs. Forrester," the voice from the other side of the world began, "my name is John Logan, I have personally been dealing with your husband's accounts."

"My late husband," Josie corrected swiftly.

"Yes, of course, I apologise. Before we can continue this conversation, I must ask you a few questions, for security reasons, you understand."

"Yes, yes, please go ahead."

"Your husband left me explicit instructions on the questions he wanted me to ask you."

For the following few minutes, John Logan grilled

Josie on Max's parent's names, the name of the farm and where he went to school. Josie felt she was on Mastermind, her specialist subject – Max Forrester; would there be a grand prize at the end?

"Mrs. Forrester, I have to add at this juncture that Max inserted this explicit message to you – Beware of Antonio Borelli, he isn't a friend! – does that make any sense?" Quite frankly, nothing she was hearing made any sense. She seemed to remember Antonio Borelli from their time at university, but she only met him a couple of times. Why was Max trying to warn her about him now?

"Now I must advise you further," John Logan continued, wavering for a minute, "there is quite a lot of money involved. The funds in your daughters' names only come to maturity when they are twenty-one."

Josie was trying hard not to overreact to the information being relayed to her. "Yes, my solicitor told me."

"Good. The will goes on to stipulate that the third fund, which was in both your names, cannot be accessed until five years after his death. I realise this is a bit unusual but I am sure your husband had his reasons."

Josie was sure he was right; the only thing was, she could not figure out what those reasons could possibly be. She braced herself ahead of John Logan's answer. "Fine, what sort of figures are we talking about?"

"That's the other thing: Max said it would be in your best interest not to know, in fact he added that you shouldn't mention even the existence of these accounts to anyone else, even members of your own family."

"I see, at least, I think I do." Josie thanked him and replaced the receiver. Of course she did not see, did not understand any of it. How much stranger was life going to get? Why had the name Antonio Borelli suddenly reappeared? More staggeringly to Josie was how did Max have a lot of money? They had always been careful, but never seemed to have much cash to put away at the end of the day. Had her husband been gambling or playing the stock market? The fact she had been asked specifically not to talk to anyone about it, she found extremely frustrating.

A bizarre thing happened three weeks later when the phone rang, not that this was a strange occurrence in itself, but the person on the other end certainly was.

"Hello, is that Mrs. Josie Forrester?"

She sighed; she was fed up to the back teeth with the ever-increasing unsolicited phone calls she had been receiving lately. "Speaking, but I'm not buying anything."

"I'm not selling," replied the amused voice. "Josie, I'm sorry I haven't been in touch but I've been out of the country. My name is Antonio Borelli; I was a friend of Max's from university." Shit, Antonio Borelli; a name she had not thought about for years and now one that had been mentioned twice in as many weeks. "I was devastated to hear about Max's accident, I wonder if we could meet to talk about old times?"

Alarm bells were ringing loudly in her head, but unwisely she chose to ignore them. "Hmm, well."

"Can I suggest we meet for a drink, if you're free? I happen to be coming down to your part of the world this weekend."

Josie had to think rapidly on her feet. She roughly remembered Antonio – long-haired and bearded, like so many other students then – but she could not remember Max talking about him much after they started dating. Why would he be so upset about Max after all these years?

"There is a pub in the village called The Bull," she hesitated," I could be there about eight?"

"Eight it is then, I look forward to it," Antonio answered, before drawing their conversation to a close.

Linda came round Friday evening to have a girlie night in; they had a lot of those recently because Josie obviously was not in the mood for socializing, so a bottle of white wine and a chicken tikka was all she could manage.

"Had a strange phone call today," she began.

Linda had just poured herself another large glass of Blue Nun. "Oh yes, strange in what way?"

Josie had to choose her words carefully; although Linda was her best friend, there was such a lot she just could not convey to her.

"Strange in the fact that ... it was a friend of Max's from university, someone I didn't really know that well. In fact, I only met him once or twice. Afterwards, he seemed to disappear from the scene. He asked me to meet him for a drink, so I've arranged to see him tomorrow night at the Bull."

Taking a sip from the long-stemmed glass, Linda smiled knowingly at her friend. "You sly dog, what's he like?"

"As I said, I only met him a couple of times, must be at least twenty years ago." Josie felt a bit uncomfortable talking about this male acquaintance, even to Linda.

"Did Max have any old photos of him?"

"Might have, I'll have to have a look."

It took quite a while to sort through Max's pile of prints. "Here we are," Linda cried, turning over a picture of four obviously inebriated, long-haired males outside a London pub. "Max, Stu, Andy and Ant, night out in Tottenham. There he is, on the left."

Curious to recall the face from her past, Josie took the picture from Linda's hand. "Doesn't really help. I should have asked him how I'll recognise him, must have changed a lot in the last twenty years."

"How do you feel about walking into a pub on your own and meeting, let's face it, a stranger?" Linda asked, knowing this would not bother her, as an attractive, well-groomed blonde; she had never had any trouble talking to men.

"Actually I was going to ask a favour, Linda. Please, please, please come to the pub about nine just in case I need an escape route?"

Linda beamed. "You didn't really have to ask sweetie, I would have been there anyway, got to look after my favourite girl." They gave each other a hug and opened their second bottle of wine.

***

"You've got to make an effort for your date." The following evening, Linda was at the cottage putting her skills as a hairdresser and beautician to work on Josie for her night out.

Embarrassed by her assumption, Josie rebuked her friend. "Stop saying that. It's not a date, I'm just meeting an old acquaintance for a drink, that's all."

The sound of the girls arguing upstairs suddenly reached their ears, and then Emma, dressed in studded jeans, appeared in the room. "Hi mum. Hey, you look really great, love the makeup and hair. You should have it done more often, you look years younger."

"How much do you want, Emma?" Josie sighed. "Nanny and granddad will be here soon, as I told you, you are not going to the pictures tonight with your friends."

"I know, thought we could rent a video as there's not much on the box."

"Ok, look in my purse but you must wait for your granddad, I'm not having you walking the streets on your own." Emma grunted a reply as she removed a ten-pound note from her mother's purse, then she stomped upstairs and turned her music up to full volume.

Josie looked at herself in the mirror. She couldn't remember when she last wore that much makeup – was it too much, she worried? Was she too old for the blue sleeveless dress Linda had insisted she buy that morning? She looked at the clock over the mantelpiece just as the doorbell rang. Beth almost fell down the stairs in her rush to open the front door to greet her grandparents.

"Hello darling, ready for an evening of fun with your granddad?" David exclaimed, hugging his granddaughter.

Peeking from behind David, June caught sight of her only daughter parading in front of the mirror. "Going a bit overboard, aren't we?" June commented, uncharacteristically.

"Well, I think she looks fantastic." David shot a warning look at his wife that made her stop in her tracks. "What time do you think you'll be back?"

"Not too late dad, probably before ten." Josie threw on a light jacket as she walked towards the front door. "Night girls," she called up the stairs, "be good for nana and granddad." Turning to Linda, she said quietly, "perhaps we should have a signal; I'll scratch my left ear if I want to leave, ok?"

Linda laughed at her friend's corny idea. "Ok, your left ear!"

Linda dropped a nervous Josie off at the entrance to the pub just before eight o'clock. The main bar at The Bull was heaving with people, mainly males who were wholly engaged in a local darts match.

Even so, several of the men looked up as she sauntered in, eyeing her up and down approvingly. Feeling even more ill at ease, Josie pulled her jacket closer around her. She and Max would often frequent the pub on a Saturday night and order one of the specials from the small food menu, but those times were now sadly behind her.

Trying to be sensitive, Jim, the Landlord, spoke to her from behind the bar. "Mrs. Forrester, not seen you here since ... how are you?"

"So, so, Jim." Glancing quickly around the room, she told herself she would leave if he wasn't there soon.

"Do you want a drink or are you meeting someone?" Jim asked.

"I'm supposed to be meeting an old friend of Max's, but he's late." Looking at her watch, she decided ten minutes was long enough to hang around – she was off. However, as she spun round, eager to leave, a tall, dark, handsome man approached her.

"Josie, I'd know you anywhere. Antonio, Antonio Borelli." He took Josie's hand and kissed it slowly, looking up into her eyes as he did. Oh my god, she thought to herself, oh my god! "Are you ok? I'm sorry if I took you by surprise."

Trying to compose herself in front of the person who she recognised at once as the very man she had seen at Max's funeral and at Castle Street, she faltered over her reply.

"Oh ... it's just nice to see you after so many years." Josie wondered if he would admit to being at Max's funeral. She certainly wasn't going to mention Castle Street because something deep down was telling her not to, perhaps it was Max's words of warning that had suddenly resurfaced in her mind. Whatever the reason, she decided to say nothing.

"Can I get you a drink – wine?"

"Yes, white, thank you."

Antonio motioned towards the smaller bar. "Shall we go in the other bar so we can hear ourselves speak – it seems to be quieter in there." Josie nodded and followed gingerly as he led the way through the red-panelled door.

For the next hour, they talked about their time at university and the people they knew. Josie was surprised to learn that Antonio had only completed the first year, dropping out when he failed his exams, much to the disappointment of his parents, who then insisted he join his father and brother in the family business selling second-hand cars.

Scrutinizing him closely, Josie believed he looked a little too smartly dressed to be a second hand car salesman —must be more money in it than she thought. As the conversation continued she grew more and more uncomfortable and wary; Max's warning was echoing through her head. Antonio disclosed to her that he held Max in high regard and always believed he had a great future. He began to channel the conversation towards Max's work, asking if he had done much travelling for Hickmans. It was just at that moment that, to her relief, Linda swept into the bar.

"Hello sweetie."

"Hi Linda, fancy seeing you here. Can I introduce you to an old friend of Max's, Antonio Borelli? Antonio, this is Linda, a very good friend of mine."

"Hi, nice to meet you, do you mind if I sit down?" By the look on Antonio's face he did mind; he did mind a great deal. Not to be put off though, Linda squeezed herself down between them and immediately turned to Antonio. "Have we met before? Only you seem familiar." Josie kicked her hard from under the table.

"No, I don't believe so," he replied politely. So, thought Josie, he isn't going to say he was at the funeral. Perhaps she should refer to it and ask him why he didn't introduce himself – but instinctively she decided it best not to go down that road. After fifteen minutes of inane conversation she felt it was a good time to leave, so gaining Linda's attention, she scratched her left ear.

"Josie, I'm sorry to be a bother but while I remember, I have company coming tomorrow for dinner. Could I borrow that brown casserole dish of yours?"

"Of course you can, Linda. Well Antonio, it was so nice meeting you again and catching up on old times, thank you for your kind words but ..." she stuttered, "I must go and find Linda the casserole dish."

Rising to her feet, she felt a little uncomfortable with such a pathetic excuse. She followed Linda as she paved the way through the bar. Turning, she smiled back at Antonio, who, although reluctant to see her go, raised his glass in acceptance. Quickly, they marched through the pub without looking back.

"Since when did you take up cooking?" Josie whispered. Stepping out into the warm evening air, they quickly found Linda's car and clambered in.

"What was all that about?" Linda demanded.

"Didn't you realised who he was?" Linda looked at her puzzled. "He was one of the men from the funeral, and the one we saw at Castle Street!"

"No! Did he tell you he was at the funeral?"

"Not one word. There was something disturbing about him. He was asking me some very odd questions; I hope I never see him again."

CHAPTER 9 – YOUNG BUTTERFLIES

Over the next few weeks, the mysterious Antonio Borelli left several messages on Josie's answering machine. Every time a number she didn't recognise appeared on the display screen, she either ignored it or asked one of her daughters to answer the phone to say she was not in. Josie never returned any of Antonio's calls, and eventually he stopped ringing.

The long-awaited summer holidays loomed mercifully before them. Six wonderful weeks of relaxation and catching up on all those jobs Josie hadn't managed to get around to. At the end of the first week, she and the girls packed their suitcases and took the early morning ferry across the English Channel in order to join David and June in their French chateau for their summer holiday.

She had always enjoyed the sea crossing, even as a child, watching the shores of England disappear, whilst looking forward with excited anticipation for the first glimpse of the French coastline. Fortunately, the sea was particularly calm and the blue of the sky was, with each nautical mile, intensifying, as the vessel made its way purposefully towards its destination.

Steering carefully down the ramp of the ship, they all cheered with delight – the drive on French soil began. The journey from the port of Calais to Ardres was not too arduous; Josie had driven it so many times before. They arrived at the abode just as June was setting the table for lunch outside, under a large shady pergola.

"Good timing, dad has just opened the wine. I think I may have overdone it with the cheese and bread though, still – I expect the girls are hungry." June smiled warmly.

The house looked splendid in the summer sunshine. It had a modern charm, a very different feel to the bungalow in Devon. The building itself was the result of a true labour of love by David, nestling as it did beside a lake on the outskirts of the town. Downstairs, a large open-plan space was enhanced with floor to ceiling windows, taking in the full beauty of the reflecting water and its surrounding area. The four double bedrooms upstairs had been very thoughtfully decorated by June, over many years, with opulent French furniture.

"Well, you've certainly brought the weather with you," David pointed out. "Have you got any plans for the coming weeks?"

"Apart from the beach, I thought we might take the train into Paris and splash out on some new clothes. What do you think, girls?" Their squeals of delight filled the air.

Oh, how the girls loved being in France. It made them feel very special, especially when they ventured into the town of Ardres itself, where they had the chance to practice their French – it was there the boys seemed to come out in their droves in order to chat up the two English roses.

Watching from a street café, whilst sipping a particularly hot cup of espresso, one warm afternoon, June remarked, "You'll have to keep an eye on those two; you do realise they are no longer children, but attractive young women with raging hormones?"

Josie looked intently at her daughters. "My god, you're right, mum. Why haven't I noticed before? Have I been so absorbed in my troubles over the last few months that my babies have emerged from their cocoons into two beautiful butterflies in front of my very eyes?"

***

"Am I a bad mother, Linda?" Josie cried down the phone to her friend later that evening.

"No, of course you're not, after what you've been through … I think you've done extremely well keeping everything together as well as you have, really I do." Linda's soothing words went some way in reassuring her. "So, what did you buy in Paris? I hope you treated yourself and not spent everything on the girls."

"I spent a little too much really, but the girls loved it and it was wonderful seeing the look on their faces. I couldn't deny them that, could I? But yes, I bought a couple of outfits, can't wait to show you."

During the days that followed, Josie threw herself into making sure Emma and Beth had the best possible time. She drove them to the beach, half an hour's drive away, almost every day, which proved a pleasant relief from the intense summer sun. The girls thoroughly enjoyed strutting their stuff along the crowded, golden sand dunes, stripping off to show their young developing bodies to the world. How Josie envied them their youth – envied them their innocence.

When it was time for them to depart, Emma was particularly opposed to leave behind the young son of the local bank manager, Henri, a handsome but gangly youth with whom she had struck up a strong relationship. After vowing they would write to each other daily, Josie managed to peel away her tearful daughter.

***

September, and the new school term at Felix Grammar stretched out before them. Work now took up most of Josie's time, engrossing her with such fervour that her family became quite concerned.

"She's working too hard," remarked June to David while he was trying to watch a football match on TV – a very exciting match; England, for once, was winning. "She was still at school when I tried to phone her at home this evening and I couldn't reach her on her mobile – David, are you listening?" A very frustrated June raised her voice to make herself heard over the enthusiastic commentator who was predicting an England win, with only minutes to go.

"Yes, yes, it's her way of dealing with her grief, she'll be fine. Now can I please see the end of this ruddy game!"

***

Before too long, the shops were full to the brim with Christmas items enticing people to spend their hard-earned money. In the lounge of Brook Cottage, Linda and Josie looked wearily at the bags of Christmas presents they had just spent hours buying.

"Can't believe it's only weeks to Christmas, still so much to do." Linda sighed as she sank down into the chair next to Josie, who was now staring blankly into the burning embers of the fire.

"This will be our first Christmas without Max. It's been almost a year, Linda. When will the pain inside me stop eating away at my heart?"

"Oh sweetie, they say time is the best healer. You must start looking forward to the future for your own sanity." Josie picked up the poker and plunged it into the flames, stabbing at the large glowing log, which seemed to be just lying there without any resistance, ready to meet its maker.

They sat in silence for several minutes until Linda had a sudden revelation and jumped to her feet. "Josie, let's take a trip to Australia, I think it will do you good to see Max's home. I'm sure it would help to heal some of your pain." Josie stared at her friend with disbelief. Was she talking about taking a vacation in Australia, the trip Max had promised her all those years ago?

"You're mad, completely mad, Linda. I can't possibly go; it was our dream, Max and I. No I couldn't go it wouldn't be right, not without him."

"Of course you can, if Max was here right now he would tell you it's a great idea. He would want you to experience the wonders of his birthplace, see the things he had seen; we could even visit the farm you've often talked about it. Come on, it would be a wonderful adventure, for both of us."

"No, no, Linda I couldn't possibly go. I'm sorry." Josie went back to poking the now cooling, grey ashes.

Linda pleaded with her friend one last time. "At least think about it, please, just think about it sweetie."

***

The following weekend, Josie took the girls on their traditional jaunt to Hill Farm to choose their Christmas tree. The lane to the farm was particularly rutted and stony, which took a bit of manoeuvring, but at least for the time of year it was ice-free. Arriving in the yard, Jonathan Oliver, the owner, who had lived on the farm all his life, came out to greet them. He was a very distinguished looking man, tall with broad shoulders, certainly, Josie had always thought, a true man of the soil.

Apparently, he and his wife lived separate lives, so the village gossips told, leaving him to bring up their two children – his daughter Kate, a good friend of Beth's, and his son Ben – almost single-handed.

"Beth, hi," cried Kate, emerging eagerly from the farm house, "our housekeeper Flo has just made a batch of mince pies, would you all like some?" The warmth from the farmhouse kitchen was certainly welcoming and homely. After devouring several pies and downing a glass of mulled wine, Jonathan and Josie stepped back outside to choose the Christmas tree, while the girls stayed to chat with Kate.

"How tall do you want it?" Jonathon asked, as he led her to the store shed. It was the same question he asked each year, and he always had the same reply.

"Six foot, but no bigger. Thank you, Jonathan." Josie smiled as he began the search through the hordes of freshly cut firs, waiting patiently to be claimed.

"How are you keeping Josie? You know, if you ever fancy an evening out, I'd love to treat you to a meal." Their eyes met for an instant, but Josie knew there was no spark on her part. She and Max had known Jonathan for many years; he had a reputation with the ladies, and she certainly had no intention of becoming one of his conquests.

"Thank you Jonathon, but I'm quite happy with my life, really I am." She decided there and then that perhaps she had better find somewhere else to get her tree next year.

***

Back at the cottage, with the tree installed in its usual place by the window, so passers-by could delight in the sparkling lights twinkling from its uplifted boughs, Beth and Emma commenced its decoration with gold and red baubles whilst Josie looked on enthusiastically.

"Don't forget the tinsel," she pointed out, "it just wouldn't look right without it."

The girls groaned at what they perceived as their mum's bad taste, but in reality, they found pleasure in her growing attempt to create normality in their home. With the aging fairy firmly installed at the pinnacle, it was now ready to be admired.

Josie woke early on Christmas morning to the ring of the phone, which was answered by a very excited Emma; Henri was ringing from France to wish her a happy Christmas. The call seemed to go on for hours; Josie walked past her daughter in the hall and commented under her breath about who was paying for this call, Henri, or his father?

Linda and Patrick happily accepted the invitation to be included in their Christmas jollities. In the steam-filled kitchen, June carefully lifted the enormous turkey from the oven, ready for David to carve. She had volunteered to cook the Christmas feast this year to give Josie a break and, quite honestly, she was in her element.

The table was full to bursting with all the festive food she had so lovingly created. June's red face beamed from behind the rather large glass of cold bubbly David had just poured out for her. He leaned over and kissed his wife tenderly on her cheek. "Looks wonderful, my dear, you've outdone yourself."

"It really does look fantastic, mum," said a proud Josie, who went on to raise her wineglass. "A toast, to 1999, the future." The sound of clinking glasses erupted across the table.

"To 1999, the future," chorused everyone joyously.

Josie turned to Linda. "I have another announcement. Linda and I, and anyone else who wants to come, are off to Australia next summer." Linda leaped to her feet and ran over to hug her friend, nearly knocking her from her chair; everyone else gawped at each other – lost for words.

CHAPTER 10 – PLANS AND AN ANNIVERSARY

Following the shock revelation of their impending trip, came the discussion over the dinner table. David was the first to offer his opinion, nodding his head approvingly as he spoke. "I think it's a great idea, but your mum and I are a bit old to be travelling so far these days, if only I was a younger man ..."

Flustered at the very idea of her daughter's contemplation, June spoke sharply to her husband. "David, you can't possibly support this." Turning towards her daughter, she dropped her voice. "Josie, I don't think it's a good idea. I mean, Australia? You've never been further than France, dear."

"I know mum, but I have given it a lot of thought and I believe it's the right thing to do." Josie had soon realised, after Linda had suggested travelling to Australia, that it made a lot of sense for her to visit Cairns and the First National Bank to sort out first-hand the trust funds Max had set up. However, because of Max's request in his will, she felt frustrated at not being able to reveal those intentions to her family and friend.

"Well I'm not going," Emma blurted out. "I've planned to spend most of next summer with Henri after my GCSEs. I'm sorry mum, really I am, but Henri's important to me."

Beth, with a mouthful of turkey, came into the conversation, "Mum, I'm sorry but I couldn't possibly go up in a plane, I've just read a true story about a crash that happened over the Alps. The survivors ate the bodies of the dead people. There's no way you'd get me on a plane."

"You shouldn't speak with your mouth full, dear," June pointed out, handing her granddaughter yet another napkin to clear up the mess.

Patrick, who had carried on eating his dinner with such gusto that his plate was almost clear, added, "Dad's already booked my holiday for next year, remember mum, he's taking me to Florida again."

"Well it's just you and me then Linda, just you and me – this dinner is really delicious, mum." They finished the rest of the meal, indulging only in polite conversation.

Later that evening, as Linda was preparing to leave, she whispered to Josie. "We have a lot to organise; speak to you later."

Josie kissed her friend goodnight and watched as she and Patrick climbed into the waiting taxi. Yes, they had, and – for once – she allowed herself a little twinge of excitement as she began to dream about their impending venture.

***

New Year's Eve came and went and before she knew it, Wednesday 3rd of February dawned, the first anniversary of Max's death. Josie and the girls rose early in order to visit Max's grave before school began. During the autumn months, they had planted spring bulbs and now the emerging leaves of yellow-headed daffodils and dark blue crocuses sparkled with small droplets of dew in the cool, early morning sunlight.

Whilst tidying up the area around the grave, pulling at weeds and clearing away dried leaves that had fallen over winter, Josie looked anxiously around her; she had the distinct feeling someone was watching them. An inquisitive robin, looking for an easy morsel, landed on the new marble headstone, chirping loudly.

"I wonder ... do you think dad can see us, mum?" Beth asked softly as she took her mother by the hand.

"I'm sure he can sweetheart, and I'm sure he is very proud of both of you, as I am."

"You're not upset we're not coming to Australia with you, are you, mum?" Emma asked.

"You'll know when the time is right for you to go; I know your dad would understand that." She gathered her daughters closer to her and they stood silently with their thoughts, reading to themselves the words so meticulously engraved upon the headstone:

'Maxwell Forrester, a truly wonderful husband and father. Taken before his time but forever in our hearts.'

The family walked slowly away, hand in hand, leaving the robin to fend for itself. Moments later, the startled red-breasted bird left his perch as a silhouette passed unnoticed through the graveyard.

A very early Easter meant the weather was still cold and damp; forecasters predicted a late fall of snow. Josie and the girls made plans to go down to Devon as usual, where David and June were busy preparing the bungalow, but a bizarre phone call from her father put pay to that.

"Hello love, glad I caught you. Bad news, I'm

afraid, we've had a burst pipe. Lots of water damage, mum's bailing out as I speak."

"Shall we come down to help?" Josie had the vision of her mum wading knee high in the rising freezing water.

"No, no we're getting help from ... neighbours." Neighbours, Josie thought, what neighbours? The bungalow was miles from the nearest house and that was a holiday let.

"Well, if you're sure ..." Josie relented, unconvinced. "Oh, before I hang up, was there any sign of the intruder you had last year?"

"Intruder? Err, no. Must go, sorry, your mum's calling me."

"Let me know how things are going, I'll only worry not being there ..." Josie concluded quickly as David replaced his receiver.

***

"Easter at home, what a bore, I miss the bungalow," Beth moaned a few days later as she stuffed her second large Easter egg into her mouth.

"You're so uncouth, Beth; just remember the saying: a moment on the lips forever on the hips, or something like that." Emma was trying hard to study for her exams; she was also a bit niggled, she hadn't heard from Henri for days. Had he found someone else? She couldn't bear thinking about that scenario. She was still struggling to concentrate when a sudden knock at the door stopped her attempt at revising. "I expect mum's forgotten her key, again! Answer it, Beth, I'm in the middle of something," she lied. Reluctantly, Beth left her position by the fire and unlocked the front door.

"Henri, what a surprise, Emma," she called, "its Henri. Please come in." Beth showed the bedraggled traveller into the warmth of the front room and into the arms of a delighted Emma.

***

Josie and Linda peered into the window of the local travel agents and could not help but notice it was full of summer deals for exciting, exotic places. Bikini-clad women were draped over muscle-bound hunks to entice the ordinary man or woman in the street to join them amongst the palm trees.

Entering this lair of dreams, they approached a young, blonde-haired rep, whose nametag simply said 'Tracey'. As soon as they sat down, Tracey finished her telephone conversation and turned her attention to her new customers.

"How may I help you?"

"My friend and I," began Josie, "are planning a three week holiday in Australia this August and would like to book flights and hotels through your agency."

"How exciting, yes of course, I'm here to help. We can arrange all your travel requirements, all I need are dates and the itinerary you wish to follow." Between them, Linda and Josie divulged to the open-eyed Tracey the trip they had been dreaming about for the last few months.

Several hours later, Tracey had finished all the paperwork. "I will let you know when everything has been confirmed. If there are any problems I will contact you at once. Do you have any questions?" Tracey smiled sweetly, showing perfect white teeth.

"No thank you, you've been very patient," responded Josie as she rose from the uncomfortable blue plastic chair she had been occupying. They both left the travel agency assured their arrangements were in safe hands.

Back at Brook Cottage, Beth greeted them at the door. "Guess who's here mum – go on, guess!"

"I'm too tired for games, Beth," Josie retorted as she removed her outdoor shoes and slipped her tired feet into her comfortable, pink fluffy slippers.

"Henri, that's who. He's come all the way from France to see Emma, how romantic is that?" Josie brushed past Beth into the front room to face the two young 'lovers'.

"Henri, how ...? Welcome, does your father know you're here?" Josie was slightly alarmed at the thought of him having made his way on his own from his hometown without his family's knowledge. She asked her questions in French as best as she could, together with a few hand gestures, hoping Henri understood.

Henri, with a playful twinkle in his eye, smiled at her attempt at his language, before replying in English. "Yes, certainly Madame, I came with him. We are only here until tomorrow, my papa has business, you understand." Josie smiled, thankful his English was more articulate than her French.

"I see, where's your father now?"

"He has booked us into the pub in the village, I think." Rather relieved, Josie asked if they would like to stay for dinner. Knowing the cuisine they were used to enjoying, she hesitantly cooked a typical English meal for the two hungry Frenchmen: shepherd's pie with home-grown runner beans she had in the freezer, followed by apple crumble and ice cream.

Later as she snuggled down in her cold empty bed, Josie wondered if perhaps she was a little jealous of Emma. She had observed her daughter and Henri all evening as they gazed lovingly into each other's eyes. She missed the romance and the love of a man, perhaps it was time she started dating.

CHAPTER 11 – RELATIONSHIPS

The following morning, Josie woke bright and early and picked up her phone. There was only one person she knew who could give her advice on dating men and that, of course, was Linda.

"Oh, hi Linda, glad I caught you before you left for work, only I've been thinking about this all night. I think I'm ready to start dating."

"My god, sweetie, really?"

"Yes, it was seeing Emma with Henri, I realise I really need somebody in my life now, just to go to dinner with or the cinema."

"What about sex? Are you ready for that?" asked Linda, taking Josie by surprise.

"With the right person, perhaps. Yes, with the right person, I think I am. However, it's been so long since I was in that scene. You're an expert when it comes to men, can you help me?"

Linda wasn't sure whether she was flattered or a little upset by this assumption. "I wouldn't exactly call myself an expert sweetie, but look, how about I come round this evening after work and we talk about it? I must go now or I'll be late."

***

Linda Maguire, owner of Hair and Beauty, 'the place women want to go to be pampered' as the advert read, started cutting Mrs. Philpot's hair, an activity she had carried out every eight weeks for the past ten years. Mrs. Philpot was in full flow, relating the latest scandal that had hit her small community, where everyone knew each other's business. Ted Field, her village milkman, who apparently had many tales to tell concerning his customers, had been receiving unsolicited flirtatious advances from a newly divorced woman, who had only recently moved into the area.

Apparently, Ted's wife, Mary, found out about this potential rival from a neighbour and surprised them both one morning by catching the pair 'at it' after the woman had invited the naive man upstairs to view her newly decorated bedroom. Ted was last seen running down the high street half-naked, followed by a very angry Mary. Now, normally, Linda would be very interested in her customer's stories; after all, it was part of a hairdresser's job to listen, and remark in the appropriate places, but today her mind was elsewhere, she was pondering the conversation she had had with Josie.

It was true, she had her fair share of male friends, more than you could count on both hands in fact, but this was the nineties and although she did not like to admit it, she was well over twenty-one.

She had met the men in her life in so many different ways. The pub always had a high success rate for her, but those relationships inevitably proved to be short lived; no real reason for this, but perhaps drink had something to do with it. She had also met some very nice men because of her job, customers who were obviously taken with her hands on approach. However, knowing Josie as she did, how could she instruct her friend, who lacked confidence in herself where men were concerned, on the art of seduction?

She brought up the subject of how to go about meeting men with Brenda, one of her young stylists, while they were on a coffee break. Puffing on a much-needed cigarette after a stressful morning, which had climaxed with an encounter with a disgruntled client, who was not happy, to put it mildly, with her new hair colour and insisted Brenda redo it – free of charge! Consequently, Brenda was thrilled when her boss asked her for advice.

"My best friend, Sue, met her current boyfriend through online dating. It's quite the new thing, cuts out all the crap ... I mean, it gives you time to get to know someone without the embarrassment of face-to-face contact. She swears by it, does my friend, it's for any age," she added reassuringly, "obviously you have to be over eighteen." She giggled. "I've just signed up too."

She thinks I'm asking for myself, Linda thought; I could take it as an insult but on this occasion, I will ignore her implication. "Isn't it a bit dangerous?" Linda queried, "Making dates with men who could be giving you all sorts of chat up lines? Do they have to go through some sort of check?"

"Yes, there are forms to fill out, but let's face it, if you met a stranger in a pub, he could be a sex fiend or anything, there's never any guarantee."

That was definitely true; Linda remembered a certain low-life she only knew as Marco. Actually, she had learned to put his name as far back in her memory as possible and thankfully, he entered her nightmares less and less these days. Those traumatic dreams from which she would awake screaming and sweating profusely under the choking duvet.

Marco had approached her in a wine bar in a quiet street off Whitechapel Road, where she had intended to purchase a quick pick-me-up just before catching a train home. It was a balmy September evening, more than eleven years ago now, and after having spent the whole day at a hair dressing convention, she really felt in need of a drink. She first caught sight of him sitting at the far end of the bar; out of the corner of her eye, she could see him making his way, slowly but surely, in her direction.

Linda, who at this time had very long, dark curly hair which seductively framed her delicate features, was used to men trying to pick her up. Subsequently, she had several tried and tested put-downs she used to deter any would-be Romeo.

Since her harrowing divorce from Shaun, she had moved back, temporarily, to live with her parents. She thought about the advice her mum had given her as she left that morning. "Don't talk to strangers," and "I've bought this for you: it's an alarm. You just pull out the pin if you happen to get into a difficult situation. They're selling like hot cakes in Woolworths."

"Mum, I'm twenty-six years old!" she had replied, incensed at her mother's lack of trust in her ability to look after herself.

All the same, her mother, Maureen, had put the small device carefully into her daughter's pocket. "For my peace of mind, just take it dear," she had implored.

It was now the end of the day; she was tired and simply needed a tonic. What she didn't need was any hassle from this idiot beside her.

"My name is M ... Marco, can I buy you a drink,

gorgeous lady?" The highly perfumed stranger began, slurring his words, while at the same time holding out his hand as if he wanted to shake Linda by hers. She couldn't help but notice the small finger on his right hand was missing.

Linda stared directly at the barman for support, but none was forthcoming, instead he carried on cleaning the glass he had been drying for the past few minutes and looked away, seemingly not wanting to get involved.

"No thanks, I'm just leaving." Linda uncrossed her long legs as she carefully descended the bar stool. She had changed her mind about having a drink; instead, she decided she would buy a non-alcoholic one from the machine at the station. Unfortunately, Marco was obviously a man who was used to having his own way.

"Are you sure I can't change your mind?" he urged. "I think we could have some fun together." His arm had encircled her waist pulling her towards him; disturbingly, she could feel his aroused manhood pressing hard against her leg.

Trying to control the fear rising within her, she managed to disentangle herself from his unsolicited grasp and brushed past him, crying out as she did so, "Out of my way, little man."

Relieved to be breathing the evening air again, she soon became aware of an unwanted presence following close behind her. She quickened her pace, to no avail, and before she could scream out, someone grabbed her around the neck and mouth, and forced her into an unlit doorway.

His urgent hands were all over her body, ripping furiously at her clothes. The terrifying sound of a flick knife, released from its storage, brought her further horror and pain as its blade sliced through her bra, cutting her right breast slightly in its quest for gratification. The heavy smell of her assailant's cologne swept over her – Marco!

"Stop, please stop!" she pleaded with her attacker as his wet tongue licked eagerly around her weeping wound.

"Shut up, you fucking bitch. This is exactly what you want; this is exactly what you came here for!" His hand left her right breast to cover her mouth once more. With his mind on preventing her from uttering another word, Linda suddenly remembered her pocket. Slowly and carefully, she slipped her hand inside and felt for the small device within. What did her mum say, just pull out the pin?

The noise that erupted from this tiny gadget brought an army of people out of nowhere, causing her would-be rapist to run off into the night, while she collapsed to the ground. Seeing her shaking uncontrollably, a passing Good Samaritan came to her aid, sensitively wrapping a coat around Linda's bare shoulder and waiting with her until the ambulance arrived.

Later, at the hospital, the police took a detailed statement, including the fact that her attacker had a disfigured hand. They also spoke to the barman from the wine bar, who professed not to have remembered the man at all. Linda believed he knew exactly who he was, but was either too scared of the consequences or had been paid off.

Whatever the reason, Marco was never caught and Linda was left to deal with the trauma that, for years, ate away at her. Not anymore, the experience with

Marco was definitely in the past and she was now quite determined nothing like that would ever happen to her best friend, not if she could help it.

Following her discussion with Brenda, Linda went round to Josie's cottage after work as planned to have a heart-to-heart on the ways of meeting men. Sitting in the garden on a wonderful moonlit evening, she poured out yet another glass of wine – this was seriously becoming a bit of a habit – as he spoke candidly about her various experiences ... excluding the one with Marco.

"Perhaps you should join some sort of club, like, say, the Badminton Club. I hear they have more men than women members."

"Yes, but most are married men only too glad to have an outlet and there's no way I would date or have any sort of relationship with someone else's husband, I know exactly where that leads." Josie sighed, staring out over the trees to the Downs beyond.

"Right, well," Linda began, "there's another way. Online dating, it's becoming very popular apparently." Linda spoke quickly as she watched Josie's face for some sort of reaction.

Josie was obviously thinking about it. "How does it work?"

Linda smiled and related her conversation with Brenda. "Let's strike while the iron's hot; let's go back inside the house, and get your laptop."

David and June had given Josie a very smart up-to-date laptop for Christmas and she had found it a godsend, especially for work. "Brenda said there are several websites, but this one is the one she and her friend have been using," Linda clicked onto the dating website and, between them, they read the instructions on how to sign up.

"I'm not sure, seems a bit sleazy, don't you think?" Josie was definitely having second thoughts.

"I'm not going to push you – mull it over for a few days."

Josie closed the lid and switched on the TV to catch the end of the nine o'clock news.

After Linda had gone, Josie logged onto her laptop again and found the dating site. After laboriously completing the form with her details, she added a recent picture from her files. Then plucking up courage, she pressed enter. That's it then, she thought to herself, my personal details are online for any Tom, Dick, or Harry to see. Why, oh why did I listen to Linda? Online dating. I'll be forty in two months. Forty, with two teenage daughters – forty. I have a good job; I'm reasonably attractive, size 14 … 12 on a good day. It's too late now. Somewhere a greasy pervert is probably looking at my picture and touching himself. Shit! She took another sip from her wine glass.

Staring once again at the website, she contemplated for a brief moment how her husband's profile might have looked on the screen – would she have been enticed enough to reply to him? This online dating craze was relatively new and had certainly not been around in their heady days of youth but, just suppose it had, knowing what she knew now about the man who had been such a pivotal part of her life, what would he have written?

Max: Australian male, university graduate with great future, seeks stay-at-home wife who can cook, clean, and bear him children.

She was being utterly cruel, of course. Grief often brings out the worst in people. Glancing quickly through the data in front of her, she noticed there were over thirty men in her local area that fell within her age range. On close inspection, many of the cheesy mug shots seemed rather awkward, and some even appeared from a different era entirely.

Josie suddenly felt a pang of guilt in even contemplating dating other men. Max was still so much in her heart; would she ever be able to let go, be able to move on? She poured herself another glass of wine and took it up to bed.

She had a very restless sleep, still unsure she had done the right thing. The only comfort she had was the reassurance from the webpage that she could remove herself from it at any time.

The following afternoon she admitted to Linda over the phone she had signed up with the dating site.

"Don't worry sweetie, you'll thank me when you find the man of your dreams," Linda said, trying to lend her support. It had always been her aim to try to instil in her family and friends an optimistic view on life and unfortunately, she felt Josie certainly continued to need her reassurance.

While they were chatting, Josie unexpectedly heard a click on the line and was suddenly anxious her girls might be listening in on their conversation from the phone upstairs.

She yelled up to them. "Put the phone down at once!"

Just then, the front door opened and both the girls entered with their friend, Kate Oliver, in tow. "Going up to play music mum, promise to keep it down," Emma called out to put her mum's mind at rest.

Josie looked puzzled. "I must remember to call the phone engineer, Linda, there is definitely something wrong with my phone."

The next time Josie logged on to her computer, she found fifteen men had already responded to her page. Glancing through them quickly, she disregarded most of them immediately - only three individuals caught her attention.

Paul: Young, forty-year-old, divorced, father of two. Engineer. Six foot tall exactly. Loves long walks in the country and quiet nights in.

Simon: Thirty-eight-year-old, unmarried. Teacher. Enjoys travel and the arts. Seeks professional companion with similar interests.

Mario: Forty-something, Latin lover. Seeks companion to snuggle up to in the evening. Been setting up my own business, now time for fun and relaxation with the right woman.

"What do you think?" Josie asked Linda after the girls had gone to bed.

"Well, some of the pictures are a bit dodgy, must have been taken years ago – just check out the outfits and hair styles, wow! I do think though the three you have picked are the best of a bad bunch. Hey the Latin lover looks a bit like Antonio Borelli," she joked, studying the face of Mario, who had donned a particularly large pair of sunglasses to impress the ladies.

"Not funny. I don't really know what to do now."

"Simple, you start up a conversation with all three; find out a bit more about them."

So over the following few days, Josie had running conversations with all three men. Paul was the first to instigate a rendezvous; she agreed to meet him in a pub in the centre of Epsom. Must be in a public place miles from home, Linda had warned her, as she should not give them any clues to where she lives, not at first anyway. Of course, it was agreed Linda was never to be too far away, and thank god for the mobile phone.

Josie decided she wasn't going to inform her parents of her dalliance into dating again; she was going to keep this to herself for the time being. Anyway, they were down at the bungalow for the second week running. Josie hadn't actually seen the water damage, but the destruction must have been immense because the work required to get it back to its former condition was taking forever, as David and June seemed to spend most of their time there these days.

For a start, Paul was certainly not six feet tall. Guessing, Josie would have put him at five foot ten at the most. So straightaway she was on her guard; if he had lied about something so obvious, was he capable of telling the truth? She had decided to wear quite a conservative outfit for the encounter, not wanting to give the impression of a female sexual predator. She felt very comfortable in her light trouser suit, meeting a man who, from the off, she felt no attraction to whatsoever.

Paul brought her a large glass of wine and guided her towards seats in the corner of the pub. He was a particularly slim man with a wispy goatee that was just about visible on his pronounced chin. She decided to ask him questions about himself to break the ice; unfortunately, he had a lot to say – mostly about his ex-wife and their two children. She tried to look interested in their one-sided conversation; really, she did, even when a few hours later, Paul was in floods of tears on her shoulder.

After handing him a tissue, she made the appropriate comments. "Obviously you still love your wife. You will always be their father. I'm sure she didn't mean to hurt you." She left him, still crying into his beer, with, "Good luck, I hope you can reconcile with your ex-wife."

Climbing into Linda's car, just the look on her face said it all. "Drive Linda, and don't look back!"

Her second date was only days later and she was confident she and Simon would have a lot more in common; after all, they were both teachers. She kept to the same meeting place and even wore the same trouser suit. Simon greeted her with a quick peck on the cheek, which immediately made her feel a bit uncomfortable. He looked older than his picture, but was smartly dressed in a grey jacket and black trousers, not the normal shabby-chic teacher look she was used to at school. He reminded her of someone, but it evaded her for the moment. Sitting a little too close for comfort, his breath reeked of whisky and tobacco, which was very off-putting. Once again, she began the conversation.

"So Simon, what do you teach?"

Simon leaned even closer, she was sure he was trying to look down her top, while his unsolicited hand eclipsed her knee. "Whatever you want lessons in, darling. Your place or mine?"

"You're not a teacher at all, are you?" She shrieked, jumping to her feet. "Pervert!" Throwing her wine in his face, she marched out of the pub and jumped into Linda's car.

"Drive?" asked Linda.

"Yes ... David Frost!" Josie cried out suddenly.

"He was David Frost, the TV presenter?"

"No! He looked like David Frost."

The following week, reluctantly she donned her suit once more. "I don't think I can do it again, Linda," Josie pleaded with her friend.

"Go on, one more time. Third time lucky!"

They reached the pub in good time, but Josie simply couldn't get out of the car, not even with Linda pleading the case for a happy ending. Therefore, giving her best friend an understanding smile, Linda drove straight out of the car park and headed back towards Willow Green.

If they had waited a bit longer they would have seen 'Mario' arriving in his limousine with blacked out windows, seen him light a cigarette before entering the pub, where he waited for over an hour before finally emerging, seething with rage. His plan to seduce Josie and become her confidante had gone awry.

He took out his mobile phone and dialled. "The fucking bitch didn't turn up!" he growled.

CHAPTER 12 – LIES AND MORE LIES

"Yes, that's correct, I've been having problems with my phone," Josie began explaining to her telephone provider, "I keep hearing this clicking sound and I've experienced some interference, like popping. I can't always get a dialling tone straightaway either, it's been happening for several weeks now. Is there anything you can do?" The operator reassured her she would send someone out as soon as possible to check the line.

The letterbox rattled annoyingly loud as the postman pushed the Saturday post through its brass flap. "Bills, bills and more bills," Josie moaned aloud as she switched on the kettle for her second cup of tea. "You up yet?" she called up to the girls. "Don't forget nanny and granddad are expecting us in an hour!"

Just then, her next-door neighbour, Patricia Wood, poked her head around her kitchen door. "It's only me. The postman put this through my door by mistake. Couldn't help but notice it's got an Australian stamp." Pat was a good neighbour, but also very nosey.

"So it has, thanks Pat. Would you like a cup of tea? The kettle has just boiled."

"No ta, I've an appointment with Doctor Daniels in half an hour, women's problems, you know. Well, better go, see you later."

Josie studied the envelope in her hand, its presence

bringing back memories of a brash Australian with deplorable manners, who had pursued her until she had finally agreed to go out with him – for just one date, she had insisted. It had been no surprise to their friends when several more dates followed, until, happily for Max, Josie conceded they were an item and for economic reasons, you understand, they actually decided to live together. Max put up no argument against staying in England after their wedding; as both his parents were dead, he felt no real desire to go home.

He had opened up about his heartbreak and reasons for not wanting to return to Australia right at the beginning of their relationship while under the influence of the demon drink, following a drunken party in some sleazy student-filled house somewhere in Tottenham.

Cuddling up to Josie later in her flat on her dilapidated sofa, his big blue eyes had misted with emotion as he revealed he was only five years old when his mother, Mary, had passed away after contracting a fever. The vision of his mother's face had gradually diminished over the years and sadly, Max had no photos of her to remind him.

He could only remember two things about her: the smell of her lavender perfume and the lullaby she sang, as he lay restless in his bed on those hot, sultry Queensland nights. His father Charlie, a farmer, had gone on to raise him as best he could with the help of an Aboriginal woman, known to them only as Annie.

As he had grown older, though, the relationship between him and his father had become very strained, the true reason for which he never actually divulged to Josie. Consequently, when Max was offered a scholarship in London, he jumped at the chance of getting far away from the tense environment his life had unfortunately become.

The following summer, Charlie collapsed and died from a heart attack, completely alone amongst the fields he loved and had worked in all his life. Annie was the one who found his cold, stiff body, slumped over the wheel of his tractor. Her wails of despair, which filled the air, would have melted the hearts of the hardest of men. In his will, Charlie left the house and farmland to Annie.

Max wasn't completely surprised about being left out of the will, as if he never existed. He didn't hate Annie; in fact, he was very fond of her. She had nursed him through his childhood illnesses and she was the one he had turned to when he needed to speak to someone about the bullying at school. No, he had insisted, he definitely did not hate Annie.

***

Josie sank back into her armchair and opened the long awaited letter. She had written to Annie months ago to tell her of Max's death, and quite honestly had given up on ever receiving a reply. She felt a bit guilty at leaving it so long but she hadn't been sure if Annie was still alive, let alone still living at Halfway Farm.

Annie's handwriting was a little spindly, making it very hard to read, but Josie managed to get the gist of it. Apparently, Annie was still managing the farm, was obviously devastated to hear Max had died, and at the close of the letter sent Josie and the girls all her love. What Annie didn't mention was Max's visit to Cairns in 1997. Perhaps she had been unaware of his trip, but Josie's gut feeling told her she was – she must have been; after all, Max had not been home for twenty years. Josie couldn't imagine he would have gone all that way without seeing Annie and the farm again.

Josie knew Max had lied about the reason for his jaunt to Australia, so it was quite feasible to her that he must have dropped in on Annie and the farm, but for some reason had also kept this from her. However, why had Annie not mentioned it – what were the two of them hiding?

She folded up the letter and placed it carefully back into its pale blue envelope. Perhaps she would get some answers when she and Linda visited Cairns in August. She contemplated for a minute whether she should write to Annie again, to let her know she was going over for a visit, but decided against it mainly because she thought it would be a nice surprise for her.

Another unexpected knock at the front door stopped her deliberations in their tracks. A young man wearing green overalls and a baseball cap, which obscured his face slightly, stood nervously before her. "Good morning, Mrs. Forrester. Telephone engineer, I was in the neighbourhood so I thought I would drop in. Hope I'm not inconveniencing you?" He flashed his laminated badge so quickly that, to be honest, she wasn't able to read it properly.

"Not at all, will it take long?" Josie looked uneasily at her watch, she didn't want to be late in leaving for her parent's house, but then again, she didn't want to turn away the engineer.

"Just a line check, I understand for noise, should only take me a few minutes." She was so anxious for him to complete the test of her line, she showed him into the lounge while she went to find her handbag. He was as good as his word. "Everything seems to be fine, perhaps the storm we had a few weeks ago temporally jolted the wires causing a few gremlins." Josie wasn't convinced but hey, he was the expert after all.

"Ok, thank you for coming out so quickly." She closed the door behind him and called up the stairs again for the girls to hurry up.

***

They hadn't seen David and June for weeks. Josie thought her parents looked exceptionally tired, especially her mum – whose normally ruddy complexion looked pale and drawn. Following a sudden heavy downpour of rain, the clouds dispersed and made way for blue skies, so luckily they were able to take themselves out onto the patio to eat their lunch while the girls had a game of croquet.

"Nearly the end of term! Have you started packing for your epic journey?" asked David jovially, giving his treasured daughter a loving smile. "Wish we were coming with you now; would have loved to have shown you the places I visited while I was out there."

"Wish you were all coming with us too, but no, I haven't started packing yet. I've only just got the suitcase down from the loft – been wondering if I should buy myself a new one."

"You're going to the Blue Mountains like I suggested? I know it will be the end of their winter, but the scenery is spectacular. It would be a shame to miss out on so much beauty," David said dreamily.

"Yes dad, it's at the top of the places to visit around Sydney. We've planned to be there for two nights, as I said before. How's the bungalow coming along, by the way, is it finished yet?"

She couldn't help but notice an uncomfortable look pass between her parents, before June replied, twisting tightly the monogrammed hanky she was holding in her hand. "Yes, it looks great – if possible, better than before – they ... they've done a wonderful job."

"They?" Josie questioned.

"Dad and the builders, of course," June emphasised the word 'builders', as if it was an impossible task for David to do all the work himself.

"Yes, of course. I hope you still feel up to having the girls for the summer after all your stress, they can be a bit of a handful these days, especially Emma, and Henri is still very much on the scene, you know. She doesn't stop talking about spending time with him when you're in France."

"We're looking forward to having our granddaughters to ourselves for a bit," David answered calmly, putting her instantly at ease. "Can't wait to cross the Channel again."

With their game finished, Beth ran excitedly over to her grandparents and mother to plead with them to play because she was fed up losing to Emma – she was sure that she would at least be able to beat her aging nana! Screams of laughter echoed around the garden, filling the air with their joyous sounds as the family enjoyed a rare moment all together.

In the kitchen later that afternoon, June asked her daughter what she wanted to do for her up and coming birthday. "Do you want a party? After all, forty is quite a milestone."

"Don't rub it in, mum. Yes, Linda asked me the other day, the twenty-ninth is on a Thursday and we're flying on the second of August, so it would have to be the weekend before."

June looked thoughtful for a minute. "Alright, I'll give Linda a ring. Between us we should be able to put a party together."

"Thanks, perhaps I should find myself a date," Josie joked.

A look of concern immediately came over June's face. "You can't do that, what about Max ...?"

"June," David warned when he heard his wife's raised voice from the hall. "If Josie wants to date, then we shouldn't try to influence her against it."

"But ..." June blustered, trying to finish the reason for her objection.

"That's enough! It's Josie's life." David looked sternly at his wife and she reluctantly dropped the subject.

***

It was the last week of the school term and Josie was once again working late therefore Beth was the one who took the phone call from a telephone engineer.

"Can I speak to Mrs. Forrester?"

"No, I'm sorry; she's not here at the moment. Can I take a message?"

"Yes, Mrs. Forrester rang last week to report a problem on her line and then, let me take a look at my notes, yes we had another call to say the line had corrected itself and we didn't need to send out an engineer. I'm just ringing for good customer relations, to confirm the line is still working properly."

Beth thought for a minute and then recalled her mum saying to Linda that the phone was ok. "I believe the line is fine now, thank you, so you've no need to visit."

"Well, if you're sure," the engineer sounded hesitant.

"Yes, thank you," and with that Beth replaced the receiver. Unfortunately, she forgot to convey the call to her mum. Had she done so, it would have undoubtedly raised a suspicion in Josie's mind as to who exactly was the 'engineer' who had entered their house that day.

***

"Hello Josie, not seen you for a while, how are things?"

Josie was shopping in the supermarket when she bumped into an off-duty WPC Brown.

"Fine thanks, getting on with things the best we can."

"I hear you're off to Australia in a few weeks," the WPC remarked lightly.

"Where did you hear about that?" Josie asked, rather abruptly.

"Was it a secret? I'm sorry if it was, I think your mother told me," she answered uncomfortably.

"Sorry, lot on my mind at the moment. It just seems everyone in the universe knows about my business, but I'm not worthy enough to be privy to theirs." The conversations she had with her parents during their weekend together, and her mother's nervous behaviour, kept going round her head. She was sure they were concealing something from her.

"Anyway, I hope you have a great time and keep safe. It's somewhere I've always dreamed of going to myself," the WPC added.

***

Only two days to the end of term and the older pupils were out for mischief because, at last, they could finally see an end to their time at school. Class 5FW had started the fracas, which involved large bags of flour and eggs – a very messy combination. The staff tried their best to keep control but even the new Deputy Head, Richard Blake, was at the end of his tether.

Richard had become an instant success at Felix Grammar School since his arrival. Josie had observed him in action in the meetings he chaired. Not only was she impressed with his organisational skills, but she also thought he was not bad looking either – with his twinkling, deep brown eyes and greying hair that hung close to his collar, she certainly believed him to be a very attractive man.

She made it her mission in life to find out more about this new addition to the staffroom from the classroom gossips, who were very forthcoming. Apparently, Richard had lived and worked all his life in Kendall, in the Lake District, where he had married his childhood sweetheart. They had a two-year-old daughter, Molly, and another one on the way, when a devastating incident occurred – his wife crashed their Volvo in a multicar pile up on a foggy motorway. They were all killed instantly; his wife, daughter and unborn child. It was a sad tale and one that endeared

Josie towards him even more.

At last, Friday, the final assembly – loud clapping reverberated around the heaving school hall. Prizes were handed out to cheers and screams as pupils were called up, one by one, onto the stage to receive the much-coveted cups and certificates and to shake the weary Headmaster by the hand. Eventually, the bell sounded for the end of the school year.

Cheering turned to crying as the pupils said their goodbyes to friends and even some members of staff. Josie heaved a sigh as she fought her way out of the staff car park, with Emma and Beth in the back on a high about their prizes. Neither her mum nor Linda had said anything more about a party so she accepted it wasn't going to happen. She convinced herself that she didn't care; perhaps they could all just go out for a meal at the Chinese in town next Thursday to celebrate her forty years of existence.

She had an unanticipated call from Linda when she got home to cancel their regular Friday night girl's night in.

"Sorry sweetie, busy getting Patrick ready for his scout camp, he's off first thing in the morning. Typical boy, he's only just given me some clothes he needs washing. I wondered if you were free tomorrow night? I noticed the Women's Institute are holding a Cheese and Wine in your village hall, I thought perhaps we could put on our glad rags and go there instead of staying in." Josie couldn't think of anything duller than a Cheese and Wine with the Women's Institute, except perhaps watching paint dry. Still, she fancied doing something to mark the end of term, so reluctantly she agreed. "Pick you up at seven-thirty then, don't forget to dress in your finery."

She asked her parents if the girls could sleep over at their house that night, she felt a bit cheeky asking them for yet another favour as they were already going to be together for most of the holidays, but they were fine about it. They were so fine about it, in fact, they even picked the girls up early to take them out for a pizza before going onto the pictures.

Left at home alone to get herself leisurely dolled up, Josie decided to pamper herself and introduced the exotic bath oils Linda had given her at Christmas to the fast flowing, steamy water cascading from the bath taps. Slowly, she submerged her whole body into the inviting liquid, which hungrily absorbed the soothing oils into all her crevices. Closing her eyes to the world around her, Richard Blake began to occupy her senses.

She imagined being held by him in a romantic embrace, which for the moment, quite took her breath away. She had been having these thoughts more and more recently, even visualizing him – dare she admit it – making love to her. Bliss ... she could have stayed there all evening, but the water was beginning to cool and her hands and feet were beginning, not so romantically, to wrinkle, so she reached for her bath towel and emerged reluctantly.

What to wear? Normally Emma would be around as her advisor, but tonight she had to make the decision on her own. Yes, the red dress; she always received compliments when she wore it, so the red dress it was. Completing her hair and makeup, she stood back from the long mirror – pleased at her reflection. Not bad for a middle-aged woman, she deemed.

Linda was bang on time, looking stunning as usual

in a strapless green outfit. "Will you be warm enough? Where's the rest of it?" Josie joked. "Mustn't catch a cold before our holiday."

Linda looked at Josie sheepishly. "Sorry about last night," she apologised before they headed off towards the village hall, "but I'm sure tonight won't disappoint."

***

"Not many cars here yet," Josie grumbled as they reached the car park, "perhaps we're too early?"

"It definitely said seven-thirty on the posters, let's get out and see if anyone else is here yet. If not, we could go to the pub first. What do you think?"

"Whatever you say." Josie was beginning to think the evening was going to be a total disaster. She was the first to the imposing front door of the hall, the very hall where she would often help with the church's Jumble Sale or the Guide's Bring and Buy. She turned the stiff handle and pushed hard to reveal the compact, dimly lit square entrance hall.

"Can't hear any sounds at all," she whispered. "Let's go to plan B – the pub."

All of a sudden, from the other side of one of the doors, a familiar giggled reached her ears. "Beth? What the hell...?" She forced open the door into the main hall.

"Surprise!" A hundred or so family and friends were crammed into the small space. Led by Emma and Beth, they all burst simultaneously into an uplifting rendition of Happy Birthday. Josie beamed from ear to ear, taking in the sight before her. Her mum and dad, her daughters, people from the village, and even colleagues from work were all there to surprise her and to wish her a happy birthday. Looking around, she could see the hall had been tastefully decorated with banners and balloons. Embarrassingly though, she noticed at a glance enlarged photocopied pictures of her from a baby to a young woman strewn around the walls – definitely dad's idea, she thought.

"Did you guess, mum, did you guess?" shouted an excited Beth, bounding up and flinging her arms affectionately around her.

"No darling, I had no idea," Josie replied, hugging and kissing her daughter.

"There's going to be a disco when Darren has found the extension lead," intervened Emma, looking for the same affection her mother had afforded her younger sister – she was not disappointed. Darren was a young DJ who was kept busy in the village and beyond putting on discos for weddings and birthday parties.

Josie started to move around the room thanking people for coming. "Everyone seems to have bought you a present, dear; we've locked them away in the cupboard next to the kitchen," June informed her.

"Thanks mum, you've certainly gone to town with the food. It looks wonderful." Josie kissed her lovingly on both cheeks.

"Couldn't have done it without Linda's help though, she's been a real trooper."

"So that's why you cancelled on me last night," Josie smiled, putting her arm around her best friend.

"Of course, nothing but the best for my favourite girl. Talking about the best, who is that stunning man over there talking to your neighbour?" Josie glanced in the direction Linda was focused. Richard Blake was standing with one hand in his pocket and a pint in the other, listening politely to Pat's latest tale.

"Richard Blake, our new Deputy Head. Would you like to be introduced?" As the words left her mouth, Josie knew instantly she was on the road to disappointment, to upset, to regret.

"Yes, I think I would. From here, he definitely seems my type of man." Linda, with Josie close at her heels, made her way eagerly in Richard's direction.

"Richard, I would like you to meet my best friend, Linda McGuire. Linda, Richard Blake."

"It's a pleasure to meet a friend of Josie's." Richard beamed, his dark brown eyes seeming to twinkle even more intensely. The attraction was instantaneous on both sides. As Cupid's arrow was released from its bow, music boomed out, encasing the room – Darren had found his extension lead. "Care to dance, Linda?"

"Love to," she said, practically drooling.

"They make a handsome couple, don't they?" David remarked as he joined Josie watching Linda and Richard moving slowly around the floor to 'Whiter Shade of Pale'.

"Yes, dad, they do."

"Care to boogie with your old dad?" Josie smiled at her dad's effort to sound with it, as they joined the others on the now packed dance floor.

At eleven forty-five, Linda revealed to Josie that Richard had offered to run her home, but only if she was alright about getting a lift with her parents. Josie assured her she was and bid her friend goodnight. Back at the cottage, she climbed into her lonely, empty bed and tried to put the erotic visions she was having out of her mind; the images of her best friend and the man from her dreams.

***

Richard drew up in front of Linda's detached dwelling and switched off his car engine. He really liked this friend of Josie's. Since the shattering death of his wife and daughter, he had become a bit of a recluse as far as socializing was concerned. His decision to move away from family and friends had not been taken lightly, but it was something he realised he had to do if he was going to stand a chance of moving on – too many memories haunted him daily in his home town.

So here he was, living in the south, where his life was certainly beginning to turn around. He was thoroughly enjoying his new school and now, well he had just met this gorgeous, sensual woman, who was occupying the seat next to him – he could feel his heartbeat picking up speed.

They unclipped their seatbelts and twisted round to face each other. Very slowly, they both leaned in closer – their moist lips touched in an open kiss, hotter than the summer sun. Richard's left hand reached for her bare shoulders, feeling soft skin beneath his fingers, his excitement intensified. He drew her nearer until their bodies were pressing hard together. Feeling the warmth of her firm breasts through his shirt, uncontrollable desire ultimately exploded urgently throughout both their needy bodies. Linda was the first to pull away - albeit reluctantly.

"Richard," she panted, "Richard, I'm not looking for a one night stand."

He looked deep into her eyes. "Neither am I. I should go; your neighbours' curtains will start twitching soon."

Linda smiled. "Will I see you again? I mean ... I feel like a teenager on my first ever date, not sure what to say."

"How about Sunday lunch tomorrow?" He glanced at his watch. "No, make that today, I know a great pub by the canal." She looked at him as if she couldn't believe this hunk of a man actually wanted to see her again, and in the daytime too.

"Sounds wonderful." Giving him one more passionate kiss, she opened the car door. "See you later then, about one o'clock?"

"One o'clock, I'll pick you up – sleep well."

She watched as he drove off out of the close, until the rear lights of his car were no longer visible. The crescent moon was high in the cloudless sky; a large ginger tom on the prowl ran across the gardens leaving his scent as he travelled. Too late to call Josie now, she thought, I will ring her after breakfast to thank her for introducing me to the man of my dreams.

***

The numbness Josie felt after Linda informed her she was going on a date with Richard stayed with her for most of Sunday. Reflecting on the situation, Josie concluded that if she was honest with herself, Richard had never ever shown any desire to see her outside school – it was all in her head. Linda was her friend, she should be happy for her; after all, she didn't know what she would have done without her support over the past year and a half. It wasn't Linda's fault she had been harbouring this secret lust for a man who she could only yearn for from afar. Linda was in total ignorance of any feelings she had for Richard Blake and it would have to stay that way.

Monday morning and the loud ringing of her bedside phone woke Linda from a deep slumber. "Hi sleepyhead, don't forget we're picking up the tickets today." Josie's forced chirpy voice on the other end of the phone brought her out of her trance.

"Yes, yes of course, see you at the travel agent's at noon."

Richard took the phone out of Linda's hand and, sliding his naked body over hers, carefully replaced the receiver.

***

The sound of the church clock chiming the hour brought Josie more irritation, simply because there was still no sign of Linda. After ten more minutes of pacing up and down outside the travel agents, she spied her friend hurrying towards her.

"Sorry sweetie, got held up. Hope you've not been waiting long." Josie didn't reply one look at her face and Linda knew she was in the doghouse.

Entering the travel agent's, they glimpsed Tracey straightaway, sitting behind her desk from where she greeted them with her unforgettable smile.

"Hi, it only seems like only the other day I was arranging your holiday, doesn't time fly!"

Reaching into her desk drawer, she took out a pink folder with their tickets and travel arrangements. "Here you are, two return tickets to Australia – flying to Sydney and returning via Cairns." She handed them to Josie, who glanced at them briefly. "Here is a list of your accommodation; I hope you will be happy with the arrangements. There is a contact number in Sydney if you have any problems." She looked at Linda and Josie, expecting some glimmer of excitement, but it was not forthcoming so she continued dishing out the paperwork. "This is the form for the car hire from Cairns." Trying to relieve the tension she was feeling from the two women, she quipped, "Of course the Australians, I understand, drive on the same side of the road as we do, so there shouldn't be too much of a problem."

Josie realised she was being juvenile; to continue the happy relationship she and Linda had always enjoyed she must snap out of it, and snap out of it now! She turned to Linda.

"Sorry, I've been behaving like a spoilt child. Forgive me?"

"Nothing to forgive, sweetie." Linda took her hand and gave it a little squeeze before addressing Tracey once more. "Now, you say there is a contact number...?"

The discussion continued for several minutes, which involved going over the schedule of lodgings that the doe-eyed Tracey had so meticulously put together for them.

"That's it then, your complete package. You know, it's strange, we don't normally have many customers travelling so far afield as you are, but since you booked, well, we've had a run of people wanting to travel to Eastern Australia to exactly the same area you're visiting."

"Really?" Josie was suddenly very interested.

"Anyone we might know?"

"I shouldn't think so ... sorry, I shouldn't have said anything, customer confidentiality and all that."

Unexpectedly, the manager of the travel agency appeared from out of nowhere and gave the poor girl a full-on glare which interrupted their conversation. Turning to Josie and Linda, he asked if everything was to their satisfaction. They looked at him quizzically, but reassured him that everything was fine, then went on to make a point of thanking Tracey for her help and left. Looking through the travel agent's window, they could see him tearing Tracey off a strip – but what had the poor young girl done to cause such a furore?

CHAPTER 13 – FRIEND OR FOE?

When Josie arrived home with the tickets, she immediately locked them securely in the wall safe – a dummy socket in the kitchen. She was preparing dinner when David and June arrived for a quick visit before leaving for the bungalow again. June stood chatting to Josie in the kitchen while David slipped unnoticed into Max's study.

"Granddad!" Emma called from the lounge, "Where's Kathmandu?" Sheepishly, David reappeared from the office to answer his cherished granddaughter's question.

So much to do, and only a week to do it in, Josie was trying not to panic. She made a list: haircut, manicure, shop for toiletries, last minute clothes, and a new suitcase (she decided she definitely needed a new one). Oh yes, locate her passport. She knew where it was, she just didn't want to leave it until Monday before putting it safely into her handbag.

The first light of Thursday morning streamed through Josie's bedroom window: there was no getting away from it, it was official – she was now forty years old!

"Happy Birthday, mum!" The words rang out again as the girls burst into her room – Emma laden with even more presents and Beth balancing a carefully prepared cooked breakfast on a tray.

"You're spoiling me, this is too much!" She beamed.

"We're also taking you shopping, mum. Granddad left some money to treat you, so we thought we'd take the train to Oxford Street as soon as you can get up."

They spent a wonderful day trawling the shops together. A watch with a jewel-encrusted face and white leather strap caught her eye and then it was around her wrist – it fitted perfectly. By late afternoon, June and David returned from the bungalow and even Linda managed to prise herself away from her love nest for a few hours to meet up with them for a Chinese meal in town.

Part of Linda's birthday present to Josie was a new hairdo and a French manicure at Hair and Beauty. Whenever she went in there, being the friend of the owner, she was given five star treatment and there was no exception on the following day … except for one thing: Linda was absent.

Linda was still at home, in seventh heaven. Apart from going into the salon for three mornings, she and Richard had hardly been apart since Josie's birthday party – in truth, they had hardly been out of bed. However, the day she was dreading had arrived. He was leaving in the afternoon to travel back to Kendal to stay with his parents for the holidays, an arrangement made months ago.

"Don't get up!" he pleaded, pulling her back onto the dishevelled bedclothes.

"I must, Josie's coming in this morning I'm supposed to be cutting her hair as part of her birthday present." She dialled the salon. "Hello Brenda, its Linda. Sorry to spring this on you, but something's come up." She put her hand over the mouthpiece of the phone, stifling a moan as his moist lips started its journey down her yielding body. "Stop it; I'm on the phone to the salon!" Trying her best to compose herself as he reached the top of her leg, she went on. "I won't be in until this afternoon; can you cut Mrs. Forrester's hair for me?" With her phone call completed, Richard pushed her back down gently onto the crumpled sheets, their two willing, writhing bodies heaving and falling in yet another ardent erotic act.

***

Stepping out into the high street later that morning, Josie looked stunning – her restyled auburn hair shone under the summer sky; Brenda had certainly surpassed herself. Josie especially admired her nails, believing the French manicure made her fingers look elegant against her shimmering new watch. Nevertheless, she was still mad at Linda for having palmed her off at the last minute. It wasn't difficult guessing where she was, of course: in bed with Richard. Right now, however, she had more pressing things to worry about; it was Friday, there was no time to delay, she had better finish packing and unearth her passport.

***

Entering Max's study, she immediately started searching. They always kept their important papers in the small safe in the built-in cupboard behind the desk. There they were: the family's passports; hers, Emma's, Beth's, but where was Max's? She was sure she had left it there – Max's Australian passport. She supposed she should have sent it back to the Australian Embassy after his death, but somehow she hadn't managed to bring herself to part with it. She tried to think back. Perhaps she had put it down somewhere? She was sure it would reappear again – eventually.

The phone rang – Linda was on the line, heartbroken that Richard had left her.

"He hasn't left you, he's just gone home to his parents for the duration of the holiday, and at any rate we're off ourselves in a few days. You wouldn't have seen much of him anyway." Josie was beginning to wonder if Linda was regretting going on holiday with her, and worried she would rather be going away with Richard.

"You're right; of course, I know I'm just being silly. Anyway, Patrick's back tomorrow, can't wait to see him. Look I'm sorry about this morning, I'll make it up to you, I promise."

"I must say, I was angry at the time but I'm over it now, Brenda did a good job. Look, we're having a family dinner this Sunday, would you and Patrick like to join us?" The interference on the phone was still causing her annoyance. "This bloody phone's still driving me mad. I'll have to call the phone company again when we get back."

"I can't say I can hear any noises this end. Yes, we'd love to come to dinner, see you Sunday."

They had an enjoyable meal altogether – the last for some time. Everyone gathered in the hallway before leaving, kissing and cuddling. David reaffirmed the arrangements. "Pick you up at nine o'clock then ladies."

"Fine, dad. Can't believe we're actually off

tomorrow, hope you'll all be ok while we're away," Josie said, looking around at her loved ones.

"Don't worry darling, you'll have your phone so at least we can keep in touch. Just make sure you keep together." June was trying her hardest not to show the increasing anxiety she was feeling inside; she didn't want to be an old grouch and say something to spoil their adventure.

It was a sultry night – Josie had just a thin sheet covering her perspiring body. She wished, oh how she wished, the journey she was about to make was with her beloved husband as they had planned all those years ago. She reached out to his side of the bed and stroked the area lovingly. She had not cried for a while, but now her tears were tumbling freely.

The following morning, with everything double-checked, Josie was ready for the off. David and June were at the cottage first thing and, as David put the fastidiously packed suitcase in the boot of his car, Josie was saying a tearful goodbye to the girls and June.

"We'll be fine mum, go and enjoy yourself!" Emma and Beth chorused.

Picking Linda up on the way, they were now en route for Heathrow.

Leaving them at the entrance to the airport, David kissed and embraced his daughter and whispered, "Keep safe, I love you."

After they had waited for an age in the long line of passengers, and checked in their bags, they passed through security without any problems. Their flight was at ten past one so, with time to spare, they headed for a coffee shop before walking to gate 45. Hundreds of eager passengers were already assembled, waiting patiently for boarding to be called.

Opposite them sat a young couple, who were so engrossed in each other's company they seemed oblivious to anyone else around them. Josie thought they must be newlyweds off on honeymoon the way they were carrying on. Their mouths seemed to be glued together; she was even beginning to wonder if they were able to breathe. Josie shuffled in her seat. "Just going to the ladies," she whispered to Linda as she moved out of her place.

"Coming with you." Linda, also embarrassed by the exhibition the two lovers were acting out in front of them, quickly caught up with her.

It was quite a relief when their flight was eventually called; thankfully, the hordes of passengers were boarded swiftly. With twenty hours of flying in front of them, they did their best to get themselves comfortable in their seats.

"Not much leg room," Linda complained, trying to stretch her legs as much as possible.

Several hours into their journey, Josie noticed the young girl rise from her seat and head for the toilets; moments later, her partner followed her. She had heard stories about people performing indiscretions on planes, but having experienced the space the toilet occupied, she could not envisage that any carnal behaviour could ever be possible.

A line of needy passengers began to form along the gangway, moaning about the lack of toilets. Eventually, the airhostess had to intervene by knocking on the door to enquire if there was a problem. At last, the very red-faced couple emerged – a low snigger drifted along the seats at the sight of the two lovebirds; she with panda-like eyes from her smudged mascara and he with his t-shirt inside out.

"Well, I'm enjoying the in-flight entertainment, that's for sure," Linda laughed. The humiliated couple lowered themselves gingerly back into their places.

Twelve hours into their flight and the plane alighted at Hong Kong airport to enable passengers, including Linda and Josie, to change planes for the last leg of their journey to Sydney, Australia – Max's birthplace.

CHAPTER 14 – MESSAGES IN SYDNEY

The illuminated lights of Sydney flickering below them brought joy to the fatigued passengers. Circling twice before the all clear to land, the aircraft began its descent into Sydney Airport. Safely on the ground once more, Josie and Linda stepped onto Australian soil for the first time, exhausted after hours of travelling. Overcome with emotion, Josie had to take time to compose herself; in fact, Linda had to steady her as they crossed the airport to collect their luggage.

Hopping onto a transfer bus, they made their way to the hotel; a four-storey building which sat right in the heart of Sydney. Pushing the revolving doors, the women were instantly confronted with a large reception area; at first glance, it seemed to be a stylish establishment a very good start.

Reaching their room, they undressed rapidly and climbed in under the crisp white cotton sheets. It was a wonderful relief to lie flat after twenty-four hours of travel – every part of their bodies ached. Almost immediately, Linda fell asleep and was snoring for England – Josie wondered if Richard usually fell asleep before Linda, so was ignorant of this medical condition. Settling down under the covers, Josie, who was a poor sleeper at the best of times, even though she was shattered, found it difficult to nod off – there was so much swirling around in her head. She said a little prayer quietly to herself, hoping Max understood why she was there.

Linda was the first to wake the next morning and left the hotel room to try to pick up something for breakfast. She soon came back with warm croissants and a small pot of jam from a little café she had found around the corner.

As the lift arrived at their floor and the doors slid open, she couldn't help but notice the familiar faces of the honeymooners emerging from their room two doors down from theirs – they looked fleetingly at her as they passed by in the corridor but showed no sign of recognition. Back in their room, Linda tried to rouse Josie. "Come on sleepy head, we must try and get used to the time difference as soon as possible, remember what your dad said."

With an outside temperature of a warm nineteen degrees, they left the hotel armed with maps and cameras to begin their day's exploration of Sydney. They had created an itinerary before they left with the help of David. Today they were going to take a stroll in order to take in the sights, and so they headed in the direction of Sydney Harbour Bridge.

Unfortunately, it was a lot further than they had anticipated. Footsore – Josie wished she had not worn her new sandals for such an epic stroll since her soles were now covered in painful blisters – and many miles later, they finally reached their destination. The sight of scores of people walking along the top of the bridge in organised parties met their eyes, but they fought against joining this strenuous activity; instead they decided to have a much more down to earth experience with a spot of lunch in an English style pub.

"Typical, come half way around the world and end up in a pub – just like home!" Josie chuckled. It had been a wonderful start to their holiday and after a bit of shopping, it was time to return to the hotel, this time in a bus. After they changed for their evening out, it was back to the marina again for a Harbour Dinner Cruise, Linda's treat – a perfect end to a perfect day.

Their last whole day in Sydney was another warm Australian winter's day. On this occasion, they decided to take the Monorail to Darling Harbour; their intention to visit the aquarium and Sydney Animal Wildlife.

The aquarium was undoubtedly breath-taking – through tunnels of clear glass they observed extraordinary sea life. Large aquatic creatures swam past them – they were in absolute awe of the size and the proximity of these giants of the sea.

In the Animal Wildlife, they had their first encounter with native Australian creatures – kangaroos and koala bears. Between them, they used up several rolls of film as they went round clicking and posing for pictures that would eventually have an album all of their own, a true testimony of their stay. By half one they were starving, so decided to eat lunch in a small restaurant by the harbour before taking the ferry to Central Quay.

Once on board the ferry, Josie nudged Linda. "Look over there, those two love birds again."

Linda looked towards the back of the swaying boat praying for the trip to be over as she was beginning to feel her lunch moving northwards in her heaving stomach.

"Forgot to tell you, they're staying in our hotel; I saw them yesterday morning coming out of their room, didn't acknowledge me though." The couple didn't seem to be quite so into each other as they were at the airport, much to Linda and Josie's relief, and more surprisingly to Linda, the girl even gave them a little wave.

"Thought you said they didn't recognise you yesterday," said Josie.

"Well they didn't recognise me ... perhaps they recognised you," suggested Linda.

"Yes of course they did, because I'm so unforgettable, aren't I?" Josie grinned.

Back on land, and with the colour beginning to flow back into Linda's cheeks, they headed off towards the Sydney Opera House. En route, Josie looked into the murky water and observed masses of jellyfish had accumulated by the quayside.

"Don't think I'll be joining them for a swim in the very near future," she joked. Reaching the steps of the impressive building, Josie had the sudden urge to run up the steps and touch its walls. Taking each other by the hand that is exactly what they did – right to the top.

"Can't believe it, we're actual standing on the steps of the Sydney Opera House. Wow, it's great, Linda, just great."

"It certainly is, last one to the bottom buys dinner tonight."

Descending the steps of the iconic building, they could not fail to notice dark rain clouds had amassed in the sky above. By the time they reached the bottom step, the heavens opened and the rain lashed down heavily, bouncing off the pavement slabs.

"Run!" shouted Linda. "This way – come on!"

They ran, looking for cover, towards a parade of shops, with their jackets over their heads trying to protect themselves from the storm. Turning into a small alleyway, a brightly coloured billboard caught Linda's eye.

Madame DuPont, Psychic to the stars - $20.

The rain was now coming down in torrents. "Well, do you fancy going in?"

Josie felt a bit uncomfortable. "Not sure if I agree with it; seems like we will just be throwing our money away."

"Come on, we may as well ... look at that rain – I doubt it will ease for some time and anyway, I've always fancied contacting the other side. Don't get upset, but you might get a chance to talk to Max – ask him some questions."

Josie shuddered; the thought of being able to communicate with Max was rather frightening but exciting at the same time. "Ok, let's do it, after you."

The gloomy entrance to the premises led into a small, darkened room covered with posters of past clients including, Josie noticed, the police, who apparently had been helped by Madame DuPont in their quest to find missing persons on more than one occasion. The tinkling of brightly coloured beads sounded as Madame DuPont entered. She was a rather tall, elegant woman of about sixty, dressed from head to toe in bright blue teal.

"Welcome ladies, would you like a reading?

"Yes, we would, but we don't have an appointment."

"No problem, please come this way." She escorted them into an even darker room, the focal point of which was adorned with a round wooden table.

"Please, take a seat," she encouraged. They took their places on the high back chairs and Madame DuPont asked them to join her in holding hands to create a circle. Linda squeezed Josie's hand to reassure her. "Have you had any physic experiences before?" Madame DuPont inquired, looking intently at the two women in her presence.

"No, neither of us has," Linda replied, answering for them both.

"Then I hope you will not be disappointed. My spirit guide is a young girl called Bella. In a minute I will begin to enter her world, please don't be afraid."

The room suddenly seemed to be enveloped with the heady scent of flowers, as Madame DuPont began breathing heavily before apparently drifting into a deep trance. Suddenly, her head fell abruptly towards her chest, before rising slowly again. A clear voice boomed from her painted red lips. "Is that you, Bella? Would you like to talk to the ladies sitting around the table?" It was noticeable that her voice had incurred a marked change. "Yes, I have Maureen with me."

Linda went cold. Her mother had died five years previously from breast cancer. Linda had taken time away from work and nursed her until her death – it had been a very traumatic time in her life. Linda's dad, Bert, had taken the death of his wife very hard; soon afterwards, the poor man had been diagnosed with dementia and was now living in a care home.

"Maureen says she loves you very much and is very proud of you. Are you still carrying the alarm? She says you would understand what she means." Linda couldn't believe what she was hearing. No one but her mother would have known about the alarm; tears welled up in her eyes and ran unchecked down her cheeks.

Afraid to break the circle, it was Josie's turn to give her friend's hand a tight squeeze. Silence followed, unbroken for several minutes. The eerie sound of a ticking clock vibrated louder and louder through their ears, until eventually Madame DuPont continued. "Yes, yes I'll tell her. I have a message for Jo or Jodie."

"Josie, my name's Josie. Is it Max?" Josie's heart was pounding so hard she thought it would leap out of her chest.

"Sid wants to send you a message to be careful, not to trust strangers, and to watch out for the men from home, they want to harm you." Strangers, men from home – Josie didn't quite understand what her Grandfather Sid meant, but she had no time to ask because all at once, Madame DuPont's body dramatically slumped forward in her chair; gradually, she released her hold on Linda and Josie, breaking the circle. Now sitting in an upright position, Madame DuPont seemed almost regal.

"Were you happy with the reading ladies?" she queried.

"I found it very moving," Linda began, "hearing a message from my mother. Thank you."

Madame DuPont looked into Josie's troubled face. "I feel despair from you, my dear. Did your message upset you?"

Josie deliberated for a moment. "My husband Max died last year, I was ... half hoping that ... he would want to talk to me, tell me things. I'm being silly."

Madame DuPont took Josie's hand. "I'm sorry, my dear, I can't control who comes through. Would you like me to try again?"

Josie closed her eyes. "No, thank you, I don't think it would make any difference. Obviously he has nothing to say, we'll leave it at that." She reached into her purse, took out $40, and handed it to Madame DuPont before rising from her chair. "Linda, are you ready to go?"

They left the building without any further discussion. The rain had stopped and the sun was already bursting through the diminishing clouds, so they joined the throng of people emerging from shops and cafés making their way back to the Mono Rail.

As they drew closer to their hotel, they passed a film processing shop and made an instant decision to get their photos developed before leaving Sydney. With an hour to wait, a quick bit of souvenir shopping was in order – several t-shirts with 'Sydney' displayed across the front, being their main purchase. Back in their room, they opened the packets of prints with growing anticipation, eager to view the coloured images within.

"Not bad for amateur photographers. Look at this one: you with a koala, how cute."

Josie looked closely at the picture and then again at the others in her hand. "What do you think of this, Linda? The same two faces seem to be in several of our pictures – coincidence?"

"Yes, it must be; who would be interested enough to want to follow us around?"

CHAPTER 15 – CROSSING CHOPPY WATERS

David drove away from Heathrow with a heavy heart. If he were honest, he would have loved to have joined his daughter and Linda on their trip. In fact, he had been dreaming about Australia ever since Josie announced they were going, but June – even with all his pleading – had stood her ground, refusing to give way to her husband.

Truthfully, June hated the very thought of travelling any further than their house in France and, frustratingly for David, had never really shown any interest in having adventures in any shape or form, in the entire time they had been married.

Driving along the motorway back to his wife and granddaughters, he began to reflect on the year he spent as a young man travelling the world. He had never really divulged too much information of his exploits to his family – his mother, Maisy, would have had a fit if he had – he only told her and his father Sid what he felt they needed to know.

It was 1950 when the boat from Dover took him over rough seas to Calais; from there, he simply hitchhiked across continent after continent, picking up casual work as he went. He saw for himself the vast destruction the war had inflicted on the rest of Europe; the obliterated towns and villages, the numerous disabled veterans begging in the streets.

When he reached Italy, he was able to get a few

weeks work picking grapes in a large vineyard. It was hard, backbreaking labour but at least he had a roof over his head for a while and three square meals a day.

It was his second day on the estate when he first saw her: Rosa, the vivacious daughter of the vineyard owner. A vision of loveliness, her long, thick black hair hung freely over her olive-skinned shoulders. Dancing around the abundant grape vines, singing as she went, she indicated for him to follow her – putting down the wicker basket he had been filling, he pursued her to the back of the dusty store shed. Now David had very little experience with women; in truth he was still a virgin and the only breasts he had seen were those in the magazines his brother Phillip kept under his bed. Therefore, when Rosa started to unbutton her white cotton blouse, exposing two enormous breasts, his emotions overtook him.

Grabbing the back of his head, she pushed his face down between her exquisite mounds. Groaning with pleasure, she hoisted her skirt above her tiny waist, slipping off her undergarment as she did so. Up against the wall of the store shed, he entered her repeatedly with intense enthusiasm.

From then on, every day, Rosa would seek him out and the two of them would gratify themselves to exhaustion, until one fateful day when her father caught them half-naked in a compromising position. The incensed farmer chased David from the vineyard, shouting and screaming he would kill him – or at least that is what David believed he was yelling – David still had little understanding of Italian, but the man's mannerisms were quite expressive ... especially the way he was brandishing the shotgun above his head.

He had never run so fast in his life, and he had kept on running without looking back, getting as far away as possible from his lusty Latin lover and her enraged father as he could.

Over the years, he had often thought of her, especially in the early days when she would be the cause of his wet dreams. He realised he probably had not been her first lover, and he was even more convinced he would not have been her last, if she had anything to do with it. Pulling up outside Brook Cottage, he sighed; June was the love of his life, but as the saying goes, you never forget your first – however fleeting.

June had prepared a light lunch for the four of them, which they took outside into the garden. Between them, they mulled over their holiday to France. The girls complained about their grandfather's restriction on the amount of luggage they were allowed to take, but then their thoughts turned to Josie and Linda, all those thousands of miles away.

"Granddad, what time will they arrive in Australia?" Beth mumbled, stuffing yet another bread roll into her mouth.

"I've told you about talking with your mouth full, Beth; don't – ok?" June remarked, scolding her youngest granddaughter.

Thinking carefully, David responded to Beth's question, "About nine a.m. our time tomorrow morning, but it will be evening in Sydney. It will take them a while to get used to the time difference. I remember it wasn't as bad for me because I went by boat; it took months instead of hours to get there, so I was able to get used to the time changes gradually."

Altering the subject, as if she did not want to think about her daughter being so far away, June intervened. "What time do you want to be on the road tomorrow?"

Without hesitation, David smiled at his granddaughters, "As early as possible to avoid the traffic, if everyone can get up that is."

***

Two bleary-eyed teenagers boarded the ferry to Calais at six a.m. on a drizzly Tuesday morning, together with their beleaguered grandparents, to embark on their two-week vacation. Car loaded, the family made their way to the on-board café for coffee and croissants. After an uneventful voyage, the drive to their house in Ardres was not a long one; they were unpacking suitcases and making their beds well before noon.

The girls loved France, especially now they had found boys. Emma was feeling especially excited about seeing Henri again. They arranged to meet in the town by the clock at four p.m., so when her grandmother suggested shopping for food in the market she was a little irritated.

"The cupboards are bare, Emma. We can't live on thin air. I want you to come with me so you can tell me what you want to eat, your mother's not here to help me ... so you must." June was feeling tired after the journey, and the restless night beforehand had not helped with her mood. She hadn't felt herself lately; she had so much on her mind, and now Josie was on the other side of the world all her worries seemed to have multiplied.

June had always been a worrier, even from a very early age. She used to worry about her mother's mood when she got in from her shift at the factory. Actually, worry is not a strong enough word for how she felt in those days. Petrified would be more apt, about how her mother, Hilda, was going to react when she saw her blood torn dress – the result of a fight at school – or her father's muddy footprints left on the floor on his return from the allotments. Hilda's fury had no bounds – she was often terrifyingly out of control; hitting, punching and biting her father, until he was black and blue – he never fought back.

As a small child, June witnessed these disturbing scenes as she cowered within the safety of the cupboard below the stairs. Then, soon after the outbreak of war, her father, James, signed up for the army. She remembered thinking how handsome he looked in his uniform as she stood in the doorway waving him goodbye – she never saw him again.

Six months later, her mother received a telegram to inform her he was missing – presumed dead. The gossip amongst the neighbours was that he was still alive and living somewhere with a French woman in the South of France. No one blamed her father for not returning; Hilda's outbursts were notorious, several had heard her shouting and yelling at him, usually that he was a 'useless lump of a man!'

Unfortunately, as soon as her father left to join the army, Hilda turned her abuse onto her only child. She would storm in, screaming June's name, filling the air with vile language straight from the gutter. When she did catch June, she would drag her through the house by her long hair, kicking and screaming. However, June, unlike her father, fought back. It was not until she left school and started work the abuse eased. Even so, she was always on her guard, avoiding her mother as much as possible.

When she finally married David, it was as if her life was just beginning. At last, she could leave behind those frightening, overpowering walls that had been the cause of so much pain, both inside and out. June kept those beatings a secret, not only from the world beyond but also from David – after all, as her mother had drummed into her, it was all her fault.

***

The market was thronging with locals looking for bargains. June picked up a chicken which had been cooked on a spit, together with lots of wonderful fruits and vegetables; it was always surprising to her that these items looked and tasted better here than anything you could buy at home.

She reluctantly agreed that Emma could go off to meet Henri, on the promise she would be home for dinner at six-thirty. When she had not arrived by seven, David went out to look for her. Recalling what it was like to be young and in love, panic began to set in. Emma, he liked to believe, was inexperienced when it came to boys – not like the voluptuous Rosa. He was praying she was safe and untouched. It was with great relief he met them walking hand in hand towards the house, unaware of the anxiety they had caused him.

Four days into their holiday, as had become his routine, David rose early to pick up the fresh baguettes they liked to eat every day, together with an English paper, from the little shop on the edge of the town. He thoroughly enjoyed this little stroll along the narrow road before the rest of the world had opened its eyes. Walking past fields of yellow corn swaying in the gentle morning breeze, he could hear with immense pleasure the dawn chorus was in full flow. Arriving back at the house, he placed the paper on the kitchen table and started preparing breakfast. The smell of hot coffee and warm bread quickly drifted through the air, waking the sleepyheads who were reluctant to leave the comfort of their beds.

"Anything interesting in the paper?" June yawned.

"Not had a chance to read it yet, had to make sure all my girls were taken care of first," he remarked affectionately, giving June a little squeeze.

Sometime later, as she was sitting down in the kitchen, pouring out her second cup of coffee, June opened the folded tabloid. All of a sudden, she jumped up knocking the cup to the floor.

"David, David!" she screamed uncontrollably, "David, come here!"

Hearing her cries, together with the sound of the crashing china, he believed his beloved wife must be badly hurt and ran with great haste down the wooden stairs. Relieved there was no sign of blood and all her limbs seemed to be intact, he was a little taken aback when she shoved the paper in his face.

"Look at the headlines! I knew it, I knew it. What do we do now?"

David took the paper from his distressed wife and sat down to scan it slowly. After what seemed like hours to June, he folded it once more and quite calmly rose to his feet.

"We go home, June, we go home today. I'll book a ferry and then we pack."

"What do we say to the girls? They'll want to know, what do we tell them?"

"We merely tell them there's a problem at the bungalow, they know we've had difficulties this year, we simply say we have to go home to sort it, ok?"

Encouraging the girls to leave their warm, comfortable beds was not an easy task; even more challenging was getting them to understand why they were leaving without giving anything away. However, depart they did. By the afternoon, they were once more back on English soil, with David driving hard for the beautiful green hills of Devon.

CHAPTER 16 – INTO THE MIST

Leaving their hotel early on Friday morning, Josie and Linda headed off towards the station in order to catch a train to the town of Katoomba, which lay high up in the Blue Mountains on the outskirts of Sydney. Chugging leisurely along its well-worn track, the locomotive passed outlying towns before it began its climb steadily up towards the picturesque mountains.

The two women sat quietly side by side in the carriage. Josie, still feeling downhearted after their visit to Madame DuPont, tried to ponder – not for the first time – upon her life with Max. When exactly had it all started to go so terribly wrong? She closed her eyes for a moment, not wanting to make conversation with her friend who was also deep in thought.

Linda was daydreaming about Richard; assessing how she could be feeling such an attachment to a man she had only known for a short time. Yes, the sex was amazing; Richard was fit for a man of his age and he certainly had all the right moves. His fingers always knew those very special places that brought her to complete ecstasy. No, it wasn't just the sex, she really liked him – was it too early to believe she was falling in love?

Linda decided she would try to ring him as soon as they reached their B&B. She needed to hear his voice again, as well as letting him and Patrick know they had arrived safely; she hadn't had any other contact since they left home. Looking out of the carriage window, she couldn't help but notice that the blue skies of Sydney were rapidly disappearing and was even more perturbed to perceive the dark, threatening clouds gathering above them.

An hour into their journey and the train slowed for the next station. Boarding their carriage were five men dressed from head to toe in outdoor gear, obviously on an activity vacation. Embossed on the front of their sweatshirts were the words 'Fat Man's Caving Club', although, Linda noted, none of them seemed especially overweight. Speaking to each other in rather loud decibels, it was obvious they were English; the men soon settled themselves down in the seats in front of the girls before turning round to engage in polite conversation with them.

Remembering the message from her grandfather Sid – beware of the men from home – Josie studied the five men carefully. Was it their intention to harm her and Linda? The red-haired man definitely made her feel uncomfortable with his suggestive innuendos, but did that make him a threat? She decided she must put those thoughts to the back of her mind before it drove her crazy. After all, Australia seemed to be full of men and women from England, either living or travelling. Was she going to be suspicious of them all?

The women enjoyed the rest of the journey, mainly due to the harmonious banter with the five strangers, who, thankfully, managed to bring them both out of their doldrums. Their carriage was now packed. Obviously bursting with the holiday spirit, the Englishmen began to sing not-necessarily-pc renditions of familiar songs, led by the only bearded member of the group, who managed to encourage everyone to join in with the uplifting chorus of a clean version of 'Waltzing Matilda'.

Eventually, both parties alighted at Katoomba railway station into mist and rain. The girls bade farewell to the men who were heading for their hostel and, with luggage in tow, made their way to the bus station. By this time, the unwelcome rain was coming down in torrents – to be honest if they had stood under a shower they could not have been more drenched. Freezing cold, and looking like drowned rats, they eventually reached their B&B. The lady owner, who lived alongside the accommodation, afforded them a very warm welcome.

The rooms were great: very quaint and old fashioned in style but clean and comfortable. They lit the already-prepared coal fire, which was soon roaring away, ordered a takeaway from a curry house leaflet left in their room and then Linda called Richard. She took the phone into the bedroom so she could have a private conversation, emerging some time later with a big smile across her face, satisfied that he missed her too. They sat together, chatting eagerly about their plans for the following two days, then, shattered from travelling, went to their respective bedrooms to indulge in their respective dreams.

The next morning, regrettably, it was still raining. Very disappointing after the build-up David had given the region. The question was, would they ever see anything of those magnificent mountains he had talked nonstop about?

Following a good breakfast, provided by the owner, they boarded the Explorer Bus which would take them to their destination for the day – the Scenic Railway. Fortunately, they had the forethought of packing warm, wet weather gear and today they certainly needed it. Climbing onto the bus, they noticed they were not the first to be picked up. Moving towards the back of the vehicle, Josie spotted the two men from their photos.

"It's definitely them, Linda," observed Josie, nudging Linda in the ribs.

"I didn't get a good look," Linda said quietly. "Let's see if they get out at the same stop as us."

They kept their eyes focused on the men, who remained on the bus until they reached the Scenic Railway, and yes, they disembarked with them and several of the other passengers. Entering a shopping and café area, Linda was able to have a good look at the two individuals, who they strongly believed were pursuing them – but with what intent, they had no idea.

"I think you're right, it is them. It's making me feel a bit uncomfortable, let's get on the train, and see if they follow."

The Scenic Railway proved an unexpected, almost vertical, very short journey to an area below the top of the mountain, but for once the clouds lifted slightly and they could see something of the fantastic panoramic vista that spread all around them.

Following the marked path that weaved its way through the thick vegetation, Josie suddenly whispered, "Linda, they're behind us. Don't look round, keep walking." Motioning to Linda, she continued. "Let's take this route, before they see us."

"That leads us off the marked track, I don't think it's a good idea, we know the whole area is full of snakes and spiders," Linda emphasised, shuddering at the prospect.

"We don't have to go far, just a few steps." Josie insisted as she took Linda's hand and guided her away through ever-thickening undergrowth.

Linda's voice trembled with fear. "Josie, I don't like this, say we can't find our way back?"

She was certainly relieved when Josie eventually came to a halt, turned and looked up the path through which they had just battled. "See? We can still see the route above us, I can see numerous groups of people passing along. The men must have gone by now, let's climb back up again."

Twisting around to start the clamber upwards, Josie's foot suddenly slipped away from her, causing her to tumble and roll rather awkwardly further down the mountain.

Alarmed at Josie's ungainly demise, Linda called out to her, "Josie, I'm coming. Are you alright?" No answer. Gingerly, on hands and knees, Linda scrambled down in search of her friend, who had, at last, come to a stop some fifty feet below her. "Josie? Josie, speak to me!" Slowly, Josie started to open her eyes, much to Linda's relief. Carefully, she helped her to sit up. "Anything broken?" she asked, anxiously.

Josie winced slightly from the pain. "No, I don't think so. I certainly feel bruised, and my right shoulder's throbbing a bit."

"Can you get up?" With some effort, Linda helped her to stand. They gazed up towards the route they had so abruptly abandoned. "Can't see the trail anymore, it's too overgrown. We have no choice but to try to find our way back, if you can walk that is?" This time, Linda led the way. Fighting through the foliage, the return journey was much harder and all together more excruciatingly tiring.

"Surely we should be there by now, Linda?" Panic was beginning to enter Josie's voice. A few steps on, the path abruptly opened up into a tiny clearing, situated at the mouth of a small cave. "We definitely didn't pass this on the way down, we would have noticed." The cold, dense mist engulfed them at that moment, making it difficult to see even their hands in front of their faces.

"Let's get to the shelter of the cave until it lifts," Linda suggested and before Josie could reply, she took charge of the situation and led the way. Huddling together for warmth against the freezing fog, Linda took a much-needed bar of chocolate out of her pocket and broke it into two.

A few hours later, they were still huddling together, chatting away, trying to keep their minds off their situation. "Josie, I need to ask you something. What do you think of Richard? I mean, is there anything I should know about him that you haven't told me? You have been a bit distant from me since ... since I've been dating him; I was wondering if ... if you had something against him?"

How was Josie going to reply without upsetting her? Should she reveal to Linda she had 'stolen' the only man Josie had been interested in since Max? That she had been having fantasies about him for months – would this revelation condemn their relationship once and for all?

Here they were, helpless in the face of the elements on the other side of the world, not knowing if they would ever see their loved ones again; was it the last opportunity she would have to tell Linda the truth? Linda genuinely seemed to be keen on Richard, would the disclosure of her feelings end the everlasting happiness her friend may well be on the brink of? Could she live with herself if she was the cause of their break up?

"The reality is," Josie began, carefully monitoring her words, "if I'm honest, I've been a little jealous ... I miss the love you seem to have found with him and I'm scared I'll never ever experience that feeling again in my life."

Linda looked her straight in the eyes. "You will find happiness again; I've no doubt about it. You're a wonderful, caring person with so much to offer."

"Flatterer!" Evading Linda's eye, Josie was satisfied she had just avoided losing her best friend.

Gently, Josie massaged her stiffening shoulder, watched by Linda who was worried her injuries needed attention. "It'll be getting dark soon, Josie; I'm scared. You hear of people being lost forever on mountains."

"Those men knew we were out here, although they probably think we've gone back on the bus." Thinking their situation over, they kicked themselves for not telling their landlady their plans for the day. It was too late now; hindsight is a wonderful thing.

"Got any more food in your pockets?" Josie pleaded. "I've checked mine and they're empty except for a pen, a coin, and my mobile phone, which is useless out here – talk about being prepared!"

Linda inserted her hand deep into the crevices of her jacket, searching for more morsels that would help keep them – dare she think it – alive through the icy night that loomed alarmingly in front of them. In her right pocket nothing but a tissue, however, when her hand reached into the left one she felt the outline of an old friend, its discovery causing her to let out a scream with delight.

"My alarm, thanks mum, I love you – my alarm!" She couldn't remember putting it in there; perhaps she had done it unconsciously, but here it was, her hero, ready and waiting to get her out of yet another tricky situation.

Gradually in the distance, drifting by way of the evening mist, an increasing sound of singing reverberated through the thin airwaves enveloping them, meeting their ears in a joyous call growing closer and closer with every note. "Your alarm, Linda, pull the pin!"

The sound the small device produced as it shrieked for attention echoed throughout the valley, startling small nocturnal mammals foraging for food. The resonance of male voices pulsated towards them. "Are you in trouble?"

"Yes, we're lost!' Josie and Linda chorused.

"Keep calling, we'll find you," a male voice shouted. Through the haze, the outline of their five rescuers gradually came into view. The Englishmen from the train were their saviours!

Downing very welcome cups of steaming hot tea, Josie and Linda were the focus of attention in the Scenic Railway café. A doctor had been called and, at last, Josie was receiving the attention she needed. Hovering around them, the evening staff were most concerned about their welfare, questioning how they had managed to leave the designated path so easily.

At last, safely back in their B&B, they mulled over the day's events which might have easily turned out so tragically differently if they had not been discovered. They both felt a strong impulse to call home, however they realised the information they would relate to their loved ones would be difficult for them to cope with so, with heavy hearts, for the time being anyway they ignored the urge.

The following day, the rain finally stopped and the mist lifted. The weak winter sun shone down on the two women walking bravely out for their last look at the mountains in which they had almost met their doom. Stepping out onto Echo Point, Linda took a deep breath as she gazed out towards the glorious sight of the Three Sisters, an iconic rock formation named after an Aboriginal legend, sparkling in the evening light.

"This is what your dad was talking about when he sang the praises of these mountains, they are unforgettable."

Absorbing the unobstructed views all around them, Josie smiled with contentment. The blue-hazed beauty of the surroundings, the tall green forests sprawling on the canyon below, was certainly spectacular. Together they had come through an unexpected ordeal, their bond now possibly stronger than ever.

CHAPTER 17 – PALM COVE

The flight to Cairns was jam packed with passengers, mainly Australians, flying being a requisite mode of travel in this vast country. Linda and Josie reclined their seats to take advantage of a short nap before the final leg of their holiday.

"I keep thinking about those two men we saw," Josie began, trying to get herself comfortable. "Do you really think they are following us, or was it simply a coincidence we were in the same place at the same time?"

Linda contemplated her answer. "I don't know, they could be travelling like we are, but there was something unusual about them; they just didn't behave like typical tourists, I didn't notice them taking any pictures or actually being interested in things around them. If they are following us, they could be on this plane. I think I might just go to the loo and have a quick gander at the passengers at the same time."

She rose carefully to her feet and started down the narrow gangway, swaying as she walked. On the way back to her seat, Linda happened to notice two other familiar faces – the honeymooners – neither of them acknowledging her as she glided past.

"No sign of our stalkers, but guess who is on board? None other than the couple who can't keep their hands off each other! Perhaps they're stalking us, just waiting for the chance to steal our travellers cheques; after all, we've seen more of them than those two men." Josie glanced uneasily at Linda. "I'm joking Josie, look, apart from when the girl waved to us on the boat, I don't think they even realise for most of the time that anyone else exists, they're too much in love."

***

The hot temperature in Cairns was a very welcome relief from the cold and damp environment in Sydney. They collected their white four-by-four hire car and, after checking the map, began the drive to Palm Cove, their base for the next two weeks. Tracey was certainly correct when she said driving on the left hand side wouldn't be too problematic, but Josie's map-reading certainly was. After several missed turns, and numerous fraught exchanges, they eventually arrived at Palm Cove, more than a little irritated with each other.

Their accommodation was on the third floor of a small complex of individually owned holiday dwellings. After struggling somewhat with their luggage, they eventually reached number twenty-four. Any niggles they might have had between them were soon forgotten when they set eyes on their spacious, self-catering, two-bedroom apartment which, to their increasing delight, even overlooked the vast ocean.

"It's great, Linda, just look at the size of the Jacuzzi bath; it'll take forever to fill." For a brief moment, they were like two young children in a candy shop.

The rest of the day they spent in getting familiar with their surroundings, unpacking, and stocking the fridge. A dip in the large, kidney-shaped pool situated in the heart of the complex was in order, together with a spot of sunbathing. It was truly wonderful to be able to relax at last in such an exotic location. As the sun began its slow descent, making way for the night sky, they took a leisurely stroll along the waterfront where several restaurants seemed to be enticing them to dine.

Back at the apartment, with various pamphlets sprawled out on the coffee table, they began to plan the itinerary for their stay. Josie, deep in thought, sipped slowly at a cool glass of wine Linda had just poured out for her.

"I must phone Annie tomorrow and see if we can visit, there is so much I want to ask her. Oh, and another thing, I haven't mentioned this before ... I have to call in at the First National Bank in Cairns. Max had an account there, I have some papers to sign," Josie lied – she still felt she couldn't reveal to her friend her private hell.

"Absolutely fine sweetie, perhaps we can do all those things in the first few days," Linda enthused, picking up a bright yellow pamphlet. "This is what I've always dreamed of doing and I can't think of anywhere more dramatic to fulfil that fantasy." Linda handed Josie a leaflet advertising a morning balloon ride, which included a champagne breakfast.

"How come I've never known of this fantasy of yours before?" Josie mused as she studied the booklet in her hand thoroughly, "I suppose I have no choice, do I?"

***

First thing Tuesday morning, Josie dialled the number for Halfway Farm. After several minutes, a weak voice on the other end finally answered. "Hello."

"Hello, is that Annie?" Josie enquired. Silence – so she felt compelled to continue. "Am I speaking to Annie?"

Eventually the voice responded. "Yes ... Annie speaking, who are you?"

Not wanting to overexcite her, Josie spoke warily, "Annie, its Josie, Max's wife. I'm here in Palm Cove with a friend."

"Josie?"

"Yes, it's me, Josie," she repeated. "I'm on holiday with a friend and I would love to come and visit you, if it's convenient?"

"Josie, my dear ... I must sit down. Josie, I can't believe it, yes, please come and visit me. When can you come? I don't get away from the farm much, so I'm here most of the time."

"Would tomorrow afternoon be alright?"

"Yes, yes, do you know how to find me?"

"We have a map and the farm is clearly marked. Tomorrow afternoon then, I can't wait to meet you." With that, Josie replaced the receiver.

Linda had also been busy making exciting arrangements. "I've booked our balloon ride for tomorrow morning, first thing."

Josie stared directly at her, not looking forward to the reply. "What time is first thing?"

"Four-fifteen, we'll have to set the alarm."

***

Car keys in hand, Josie insisted that on this occasion,

she was going to drive and Linda was going to navigate. This arrangement fared much better than the day before and, in next to no time, they were standing in line at the First National Bank in Cairns. Reaching the counter, Josie asked if it was possible to speak to John Logan.

"And your name is, please?" enquired the bank teller.

"Mrs. Josie Forrester."

"Thank you, I'll just buzz through to see if Mr. Logan can speak to you, would you like to take a seat?"

John Logan emerged moments later, arm outstretched, eager to shake her by the hand. "Mrs. Forrester, a pleasure to meet you in person."

"Likewise. Mr. Logan, this is my friend, Linda Maguire."

"Delighted to meet you. Please call me John, Mrs. Forrester, we like to be on first name terms here."

With the niceties over, John led Josie into his office whilst Linda waited patiently in the comfortable lounge provided for the bank customers.

Looking around the lavish room, she observed, apart from the awards that were strewn about the walls, it was decorated with fine, dark wood furniture. In the corner, a large drinks cabinet stood, apparently waiting to offer a drink to customers and bank employees alike. Josie certainly could see where some of the bank profits were being spent.

"Mrs. Forrester, how can I be of help?" John began, sitting back in his black padded swivel chair, twiddling a red pencil between his fingers – a habit Josie found very irritating at the best of times. Craning her neck, she could see Max's file open on his desk.

"I've come because I was wondering if there was anything else you can tell me about my husband's visit to your bank?"

Glancing down at the file, he sighed. "I'm sorry; I told you everything concerning the trust funds. I'm not sure what more I can tell you."

Josie wasn't satisfied with this answer. Did this being before her not realise she had come half way around the world to try to understand more about her husband and his motive for making his will? She tried to keep calm.

"I know it was a while ago, but can you remember anything about my husband's mood, for instance? How did he seem to you?"

John finally put his pencil down. "When your husband came to see me, he seemed quite agitated. He was eager to get his finances in order, almost, I have to say, to the point of desperation." John looked at Josie, appearing to deliberate carefully his next words. "Mrs. Forrester, I think he was scared, it was even possible he feared for his life." Josie jumped to her feet and began pacing the room. "Sometimes," John continued, "our jobs are like doctors; customers confide in us things they can't or won't tell other people, especially when they are writing their wills." Josie was becoming more and more distressed at these disclosures; tears welling up in her eyes. John handed her several tissues. "I'm sorry if I've upset you, Mrs. Forrester, can I get you a drink?"

"No, thank you, I'm driving." Trying to get this new revelation clear in her head, she demanded, "Why did you never reveal his state of mind to the authorities? You know he died following a hit-and -

run, this could have been important."

He leaned forward in his chair. "Quite frankly, Mrs. Forrester, until now no one has ever asked me and it was months after his death that your solicitor contacted the bank. Max's frame of mind never came into our conversations."

"I see, well thank you for being so candid, and thank you for your time." Perhaps he was not a cold-hearted mortal as she had first thought.

Seeing her friend obviously distressed, Linda offered to drive back to Palm Cove. Josie was very quiet for the rest of the day. Linda, although oblivious to the conversation that had taken place in John's office, told her she was there for her if she wanted to talk.

Going over and over again in her head were the words Max feared for his life; the question was why, and from whom? Then it came to her: why had she not contemplated the idea before? Could the unthinkable have happened, had Max been murdered? She shuddered at the enormity of the idea and made the decision to go straight to the police with this new information as soon as she got home.

Perhaps she should get John Logan to write a letter, outlining his conversation with Max. Yes, she decided, that was a good idea. In the meantime, she wasn't going to let it affect the rest of their stay, it wasn't fair to Linda; after all, Max was dead, nothing she did now could ever bring him back. That night, as she had done on several other occasions since arriving in Palm Cove, she tried to call her parent's home in France. Still no answer – should she be worried?

***

At four-fifteen the following morning, two bleary-eyed women boarded a bus with other comatose humans for their ride to the balloon launch site. Josie was beginning to wonder if she was really up for it – but it was too late to change her mind now. Too late for excuses. Before them loomed an amazing spectacle. In the morning darkness, shadows of several enormous balloons rose up before them. The deafening noise of air, inflating these giants of the sky, vibrated in their ears. As the sun rose and rays of light flooded the field, they were organised into groups. Thankfully, the friends were together.

Neither of them had ever given any thought about how to get into the basket that hung below the colourful monster. Everyone in the party had to show they could climb into the sizeable wicker box without any assistance. Apparently, it was a safety thing. Both Linda and Josie managed it, eventually, but their dignity took a bit of a bashing. Their spirits were raised though, as they tumbled into the basket and came face to face with the pilot – Indiana Jones's twin brother!

While the balloon drifted higher and higher into the cloudless deep blue sky, everyone marvelled at the terrain far below. Josie wondered if they were flying anywhere near Halfway Farm. Were they floating over the fields where, as a boy, Max would have been running and playing? They had a brilliant flight, took numerous pictures, and landed safely without too much bumping on the uneven ground. Everyone in the group was expected to help with gathering up the balloon, before being whisked away from the landing site. The morning activities ended with breakfast and a glass of bubbly.

Following a brief rest, the girls set off along the Bruce Highway to drive the thirty miles south towards Halfway Farm. Josie couldn't help but think about what they would find when they got there. She imagined a rundown shack, in the middle of nowhere, a few chickens scratching about and perhaps a barking dog on a tether. Max's father had died such a long time ago; she supposed Annie would have struggled to keep the farm going on her own. She was worrying she would find her living in squalor.

Three quarters of an hour into their journey, they pulled over into a petrol station. While Linda was filling up the tank, Josie popped into the small shop to buy more bottles of water. Glancing out of the large display window, she couldn't help but notice another car had pulled up several feet before the pumps.

Squinting against the glaring sunlight, she took a deep breath. She couldn't be one hundred percent sure but, sitting in the silver car and looking a little shifty, were, she believed, their stalkers! Josie quickly paid for the petrol and her purchases, then exited the shop without drawing attention to the fact she had seen the men. Climbing into their vehicle, she told Linda not to turn round.

"I think we have company, the two men in the car behind us."

Alarmed at the prospect of their continued surveillance, Linda re-entered the highway, keeping a close eye on her rear view mirror.

"Whoever is in that car didn't need petrol and they certainly didn't go in the shop," Josie confirmed.

"Right, let's take the next turning and see if they do the same," replied Linda, apparently excited at the thought of a possible car chase.

Entering a small town, Linda slowed for the overhead traffic lights. The very moment they changed to green, she put her foot down hard on the accelerator and took a sharp left, causing the wheels to squeal with excitement. Weaving in and out of unknown streets like fugitives on the run, hoping the local police didn't spot them, they finally re-joined the highway.

"Any sign?" Linda demanded, the adrenaline now pumping through her body.

Josie looked around them. "Not so far, let's hope we gave them the slip."

Were their imaginations running wild? Were those men following them, or were they simply being paranoid? Whatever their fears, they were alone now, driving the last few miles before the turn off for Halfway Farm.

Josie was the one to see the signpost first. "There it is, on the right, Linda. Slow down!"

Manoeuvring along the twisting road taking them to the farm, anticipation was rising within Josie. After several miles on the uneven track, the road finally opened up into a large clearing on which stood Halfway Farm, tall and proud, in front of a rising forest of evergreens.

"Wow!" exclaimed Linda.

CHAPTER 18 – ANNIE

A large, bronze metal sign on the side of the entrance gate read: Halfway Farm, Rainforest Horseback Adventures. The long, straight track stretching up before them to the house was lined with newly painted, wooden-fenced paddocks, in which several contented horses and foals were grazing side by side, or just simply standing quietly together swishing their tails under the shade of the overhanging trees that eclipsed the drive. Alongside the prominent two-storey farmhouse stood several outbuildings, including a long row of smart stables and an impressive hay barn. Linda slowed, so they could try to take in the sight that had completely blown them away.

"It's fantastic. Max always led me to believe his father struggled to make a living." Continuing along the dirt track to the farmhouse, lingering slightly in order to take everything in, they could see the front door of the house opening and the figure of a woman emerging, her arms wide open in greeting.

Annie was nothing like the image Josie had built up in her mind. For a start, she was much younger, probably in her early fifties with long black hair tied back into a neat ponytail – it was also obvious from her features she was not pure Aborigine. Sobbing uncontrollably, Annie threw her arms around an overwhelmed Josie, almost sending her flying.

"Josie, Josie, I always dreamed this day would

come, welcome."

So Linda didn't feel left out of all the emotion, Josie quickly introduced her to Annie, who afforded her the same enthusiastic treatment. Clinging to each other as if long lost friends, they commenced the climb up the five porch steps that rose central to the timber building. The three women entered the cool space beyond the door, a sizeable sitting area dominated by an imposing wooden staircase.

Showing the girls into her rustic kitchen, she offered them a much-appreciated glass of cold homemade lemonade. Drinks in hand, Annie led them into yet another room, this time at the back of the house; a cooler, darker area, where they eased themselves down onto two large, brown leather sofas.

"Sorry I sounded a bit out of it when you phoned yesterday, I'd been up half the night with one of my mares that was having trouble foaling," Annie announced apologetically as she kicked off her dusty trainers.

"I'm sorry if I woke you," Josie returned. "Is the mare ok?"

"Yes, she's fine, gave birth to a gorgeous filly. I'll show her to you later."

Putting down her empty glass, Linda broke into the conversation. "Well Annie, this is quite a place you have here, it's very impressive."

Annie smiled appreciatively. "Thank you; it was always my dream to introduce horses to the farm. It has taken a lot of hard work, I can tell you, but I'm very proud of everything we've managed to do."

Josie rose to her feet and walked towards something that had caught her eye. Picking up a gold-coloured encrusted photo frame taking pride of place on top of a small grand piano, situated close to an open window, she turned to Annie.

"Is this a picture of Max and his father?" she asked, examining the photo closely.

"Yes, it was taken the year before Max left for England; you can see where Max got his good looks from, can't you?" Annie seemed to be lost in the past for a brief moment, remembering the two men who had once been the centre of her universe.

Josie was puzzled. The happy scene leaping from the image had certainly taken her by surprise; the men were standing arm in arm, smiling broadly to the camera. This was, she contemplated, not the look of the strained relationship Max had always insisted he had with his father.

"They look very content with each other in this picture. Did they normally get on well?"

Annie took the photo from Josie and held it tenderly in her hands. "They do look happy, don't they? This is exactly how I like to remember them. Regrettably, the six months before Max left were, to be honest, a bit strained. They had a falling out, you see, and afterwards rarely spoke a civil word to each other. In fact, they could hardly bear to be in the same room ... it was a very uncomfortable time." Annie didn't elaborate further, leaving Josie wondering exactly what the two men had quarrelled about. She hoped she would have a chance to ask Annie more about their relationship later.

"Have you any more photos of Max? I would love to see them if you have."

From out of nowhere, Annie produced album after album of photos, lovingly catalogued, mainly of Max from a bouncing baby to a strapping teenager, but the most mesmerizing photos were of Annie herself – a tiny waif who, over time, had blossomed into the attractive, middle-aged woman who now sat before them.

"Annie, how did you get the job working for the Forrester's? Did your parents work for them too?

Annie looked melancholy for a moment, rubbing her hands together as if not quite sure what to say. Josie hoped her question had not been too intrusive; the last thing she wanted to do was to upset her.

"I knew nothing of my family until a few years ago when I was allowed to read my government files, and from them I managed to trace my mother's sister. I went to visit her and she told me everything. Mum had only died a few years before, I must admit that fact has been haunting me." Annie wiped a tear from her eye.

"Annie, if it's too painful, then please, you don't have to tell us," Josie said, handing her a tissue.

"No, its fine, I want to tell you. My mother was an Aboriginal woman who had been a slave for a rich white landowner. He turned out to be a monster of a human being, and sadistically raped her countless times. When she found out she was pregnant, her fear was for me. You see, the Australian government had ruled at the time that mixed-race babies should be removed from their families; apparently my mum did all she could to keep me hidden."

"Then, one horrifying day when I was two years old, a day my aunt said still troubles her, two nuns arrived at the dilapidated shack mum and I shared with my grandparents and took me forcibly from my screaming mum to live at a Mission hundreds of miles away from my home. I became part of the stolen generation, one of the darkest chapters in Australian history. Of course, my Mission life I remember very well. I suffered mental and physical abuse like the other young souls. I was often beaten and worked until I collapsed with exhaustion. On the positive side, I was taught to read and write."

"Oh, I'm so sorry, Annie, it's a heart-wrenching story, but how did you end up here?" Josie asked.

"When I was sixteen, I was summoned to the priest's office together with three other girls of about the same age. We were paraded like cattle in front of a bereaved Charlie. He picked me out from the line up, I think, to be honest, because I was the whitest girl there. Racism was rampant at that time, and Charlie was no exception. He didn't utter a word, just beckoned for me to follow him. I was devastated at not even having a chance to say goodbye to the other children who had been my family for fourteen years."

"So Charlie wanted someone to look after his child, I'm guessing. How old was Max then, about six?" Josie surmised.

"Yes, he was a lovely boy, quite clingy; he really missed his mother. Charlie just left me alone to take care of him and the house. I have to say Charlie was always a kind and considerate man to me and after a period of time, even encouraged me to go to school. From there I went on to college, to study Farm Management, and look at me now, I have a thriving business. Who'd have thought my life would have turned out so well," Annie exclaimed, jumping to her feet. "Do you fancy a drink? Something a bit stronger? I could certainly do with one." She opened a drinks cabinet and poured out three small whiskies.

"Annie, look, I'm sorry if I've upset you..." Josie

began.

"It's just been a while since I've thought about my past, that's all. I'm fine, really I am. Look around you: it all came good in the end."

***

Annie sighed to herself; there was so much more she could tell – personal stuff about Max, which would mean Josie would look at her through different eyes and Annie definitely didn't want that to happen.

She thought about how he had grown from a young boy to a young man of eighteen, whilst the years between them seemed to diminish, after all she was only ten years his senior. The friends he used to bring back to the farm were always making some sort of sexual comments to her, making her feel more than a little uncomfortable.

She remembered clearly that last autumn in '78, before Max left for England. The heavy rains, which had plagued the previous months, had eased, and he and his father were busy on the farm. On one particular Saturday, Charlie had left soon after breakfast to drive into Cairns in order to pick up a part for his tractor, leaving Max with a list of jobs to do while he was away.

After toiling hard in the fields for several hours he had worked up quite a sweat, so he downed his tools and drove back to the house with the intention of taking a much-needed shower. While he was making his weary way towards his bedroom, Annie was emerging from the bathroom with her body wrapped in a soft white cotton towel.

Embarrassed, they both tried to avoid each other's

gaze, but as they tried to pass on the landing, Annie slipped on the wooden floor and fell into Max's arms, her towel sliding down her still damp, naked form, exposing her pert breasts.

Mortified by the situation she found herself in, and wincing with the pain now shooting through her ankle, Annie tried desperately to move away from his grasp but without much success. Ignoring her protests, Max gallantly swept her up in his strong, bare arms and this time their eyes met with an unavoidable, yearning desire; they simply could not help themselves, their excited loins were totally overtaken with pure lust.

Dropping onto Annie's bed, they kissed and caressed each other with such eagerness that Max worried his passion would out before he could perform the completing act – which they were obviously both desperately desiring. Their heaving bodies finally came together with an explosion of ecstasy that brought them complete satisfaction.

They lay together for a while, still holding each other, enjoying the tantalising feeling of their exposed skin. Afterwards, the incredible guilt about what they had just done overwhelmed them. They both vowed it must never happen again.

From that moment on, Annie tried to avoid Max as much as possible and he, in turn, threw himself fully into his schoolwork. However, sexual desire is a strong emotion, especially for a young man, and ignoring it eventually became nigh on impossible. Whenever they were alone, they made love; erotic, animal love – no part of the house or farm was off limits.

Until one ill-fated day when Len Dixon, their near

neighbour, saw them lying together in the top field and conveyed his disgusted sighting to a speechless Charlie. Annie had never seen Charlie in such a rage; had never before witnessed the violence that followed. When he had finished the brutal beating of his only son, the two men never spoke to each other again.

It was with immense relief, therefore, that Max received the letter offering him a place at the London School of Economics in England. He jumped at the opportunity of getting well away from the farm; not away from Annie, no, he told her he would miss her deeply, but away from his dad who was making his life unbearable. Before he left, however, he and Annie had a final passionate moment together – simply to say goodbye.

That part of her life was in the past and that's exactly where it had to stay now.

***

Shuffling through more family snaps, Josie picked up a photo of Annie with a contented looking baby in her arms. "Whose baby is this, Annie?" she enquired.

Annie looked proudly at the print. "My son John, wasn't he beautiful?" He certainly looked a bonny boy with gorgeous blonde curls.

"When was he born?" Josie queried, looking down at the tiny chap who looked very familiar.

"April 1979, the year Charlie died." Linda and Josie exchanged glances. "I don't know if Max ever told you, he wasn't aware of it himself until years later, but Charlie married me before John was born. He told me he wanted to make things right." So, Max had a half-brother. Things were beginning to make sense at last; Annie was Charlie's wife and that was why she was left the farm.

The burning question on Josie's lips was how a young widow had managed, against all odds, to turn the farm around and make such a success of it, while bringing up a baby all on her own, but first she wanted to hear whether Max had been to see her when he was in Cairns. Looking directly at Annie, she broached the subject. "Annie, were you aware Max visited Cairns in '97? Did he come here to the farm?"

Annie, deliberating her answer, looked about her sadly, tears building once again in her deep brown eyes. "Yes, he came here. It was wonderful to see him after almost twenty years, he wanted to meet John and check on his investment."

Josie was startled at this last statement. "His what? Investment? I don't understand."

Linda began to feel slightly uncomfortable about the direction the conversation seemed to be going. Rising to her feet, she volunteered, "Would you like me to step outside, Josie, while you discuss family affairs?"

"There's no need for you to leave, Linda," Josie insisted, beckoning her to resume her seat on the sofa.

"You really don't know?" Annie seemed genuinely stunned that Josie had no knowledge of her and Max's business partnership. She continued, "Well, for years Max sent me money every month to invest in the farm, that's how I've managed to build it up, with Max's help. I'm sorry, I didn't realise he had kept this from you."

Secrets, so many bloody secrets – when will it all

come to an end? Once again, money raised its ugly head – where the hell was it all coming from? How much had he sent over the years? It must have been a substantial amount to have helped develop the farm to such an impressive grandeur. More importantly, why did he feel the need to help Annie and why did he not tell her what he was doing?

All of a sudden, a silhouette appeared in the doorway. A tall, broad-shouldered youth with piercing blue eyes who was the spitting image of Max. The familiar sight of John Forrester unsettled Josie for a brief moment.

"John, come and meet Josie and her friend, Linda." Annie, obviously relieved at the appearance of her only son, slipped her shoes back on and leapt to the door, encouraging the seemingly shy young man to mingle with their visitors. "Is the trek going smoothly?" Annie asked, trying to put him at ease.

"Yes mum, left them at the creek setting up camp a few hours ago."

Annie turned back to Josie and Linda. "Once a week, we run a three day trek where riders sleep under canvas for two nights; it's very popular with holiday makers. They left yesterday morning and aren't due back until tomorrow night. John had to get back, has a date, don't you, dear?" She beamed dotingly at her son, who was obviously embarrassed by his mother's disclosure. They all sat and talked for a while – Josie studying John closely. He certainly looked like a member of the Forrester family; he even had a mouth and smile that reminded her of Emma.

Although Linda was enjoying this family reunion, quite frankly, she was getting a little restless. "How about showing me around the farm, John? I could do with stretching my legs."

"Good idea," Annie agreed immediately. Before the young lad had a chance to answer, Linda was at the door on her way out to the open air. Annie turned to Josie. "Come on, we can carry on talking while I prepare dinner. You must be starving."

Ambling around the estate, Linda tried to engage John into conversation. "I expect it was quite difficult for you, growing up without a dad around." She hoped she wasn't overstepping the mark, being over-familiar with her questions.

"I suppose I never knew him, so I never missed him. Anyway, Scott has been in my life for as long as I can remember."

"Scott?"

"Yes, Scott Jones, the farm manager. He and mum have been a sort of item for years, don't think they will ever marry though."

So, Annie had a fella, did she? Well good for her. Linda knew only too well what it was like to be without a man in her life, and for just a second she thought once again of Richard. She hadn't dared mention this to Josie, but she was actually beginning to count the days until she saw him again. She was enjoying their trip, but Richard ... well.

Two sleek black Labradors unexpectedly bounded up to them, barking and wagging their tails enthusiastically; they obviously adored John, hanging on his every command. Continuing the tour of the estate, with the animals at their heels, they arrived at the field behind the house: a large open area, the top end of which was the commencement of the forest beyond. A wooden hut lay to the left, into which John disappeared before re-emerging a moment later clutching a couple of ornate boomerangs.

"Ever thrown one of these?" He grinned cheekily.

"Not lately," Linda hesitated, "but I've a feeling I'm going to."

"We use this field for demonstrations, and then our clients are let loose. It's actually a lot harder than it looks, so don't get too despondent."

In fact, Linda proved a very good pupil. After John's initial demonstration, where the boomerang almost circled the perimeter of the entire field, coming skilfully back to the hand of its thrower, it was Linda's turn. Following a couple of false starts, she managed to throw the highly decorated aboriginal weapon in a small circle, impressing John so much he told her she could keep it – to practise with when she got home.

Back in the kitchen, Annie was busy preparing a salad to accompany the T-bone steaks she removed from the fridge, ready to be thrown on the barbecue which was now well underway. Annie seemed relieved to have Josie to herself for a bit.

"Josie," she began hesitantly, "there was another reason Max came to the farm." Josie stopped chopping the cucumber at once to give Annie her full attention. "He came to give me something he wanted me to look after. He told me he would come back and collect it one day, but of course now that day will never come. So, I think I should give it to you."

Josie was intrigued. Annie guided her back to the room with the piano. Once again, she picked up the picture frame of Max and his father, but this time she turned it over, and carefully opened the back to reveal a single floppy disk. Holding it up to the light, she explained, "I've no idea what's on it, Max refused to disclose its contents – said it was better I didn't know. I've never tried to load it onto my machine; I thought you might like to. I have a laptop you could take away with you – if you want to, that is?"

Josie took the disk cautiously from Annie. For Christ's sake, what next? A growing money mountain and now a mystery disk which might reveal even more secrets.

"Another surprise – seems to be the order of this holiday. Yes, thanks, I'd love to borrow your laptop."

Annie was pleased to be seeing the back of the little item which had been troubling her ever since she learned of Max's death.

"I was thinking perhaps you might like to come and stay here for a few days, I've plenty of room and, well, let's face it, we might never have another chance to talk together."

Josie did not take long to consider the proposal. "What a great idea. I'll have to mull it over with Linda first, of course, but if she agrees, we'll go back to our apartment, get a few things, and return here tomorrow."

The T-bone steaks hit the mark – a perfect end to an extraordinary day. Annie and John stood on the porch, waving goodbye, as Josie and Linda drove off back along the drive towards the vibrant orange and red sunset, now impressively dominating the far horizon. The women wondered what new revelations would be in store for them when the new sun rose from its turbulent sleep the following morning.

CHAPTER 19 – DISCLOSURES

Night fell on the Bruce Highway as the headlights of their car gleamed powerfully through the ever-darkening sky, guiding its passengers onwards to Palm Cove. Deliberating the day's disclosures, Linda agreed it was necessary to revisit Halfway Farm as it still held so many unanswered questions.

Drawing comfort from the illuminating lights, growing more intense as they approached the populated area of the town, they stopped at a small, late night shop to pick up a few necessary supplies. Since they had been in Australia, they had deliberately not bought an English paper mainly, as Linda had emphasised, because the cost was grossly inflated abroad and the news was always several days out of date anyway. Nevertheless, tonight she decided to give in and picked up Tuesday's issue of the Daily Mail to give her something to read while they were staying at the farm.

Back at the apartment, Josie enthusiastically turned on the taps for the Jacuzzi and sat back, patiently waiting for the immense void to be filled, while Linda flicked the kettle on for a much-needed cup of tea. Sprawling, rather unladylike, on one of the two chairs occupying the lounge area, Linda picked up the paper and studied the headlines carefully.

DRUGS GANG BOSS BOUND OVER
Police have successfully charged the head of the Borelli Crime

Syndicate, Giorgio Borelli, with running an illicit drugs ring and money laundering. Borelli, as reported by this paper, was arrested last Thursday following years of police investigation and will appear in court today. Chief Inspector Wainwright of New Scotland Yard has been reported as saying that several members of the public have already come forward with important new evidence following the police appeal last week. Giorgio Borelli's sons, Marco and Antonio, wanted in connection with several unsolved murders and rapes around the capital, were still on the run last night - the police fear they may have already left the country. Chief Inspector Wainwright added that these men are extremely dangerous and should not be approached at any cost.

Linda could feel her heart thumping in her chest and her stomach seemed to be turning summersaults. A surge of utter panic engulfed her and then from deep within came an inhumane cry.

"JOSIE! JOSIE! ANTONIO BORELLI!"

Leaping from the soothing waters that had only just begun to envelope her aching body, Josie reached for the towelling robe, draped casually over the bathroom chair, and propelled herself out of the steaming room to console her best friend, who sounded as if she were in profound distress.

"Linda, whatever's the matter? You look as if you've seen a ghost."

Linda thrust the paper in Josie's direction. "Read it; read the lead story!"

With a growing look of horror emerging on her face, Josie's eyes scanned the article closely, absorbing the familiar name it contained. In a complete whirl, trying to take on board the significance of this latest discovery, she felt the need to hug Linda for comfort;

in fact, in this particular instance this gesture benefited both of them.

Antonio Borelli, son of a drugs baron – Josie thought her head would explode in a million pieces. A murderer, a rapist! They couldn't believe they had both been voluntarily in this depraved man's company, albeit for a short time.

Josie decided now was the time to disclose everything she knew to Linda; after all, unknowingly, she might have dragged her friend into an extremely dangerous situation. Linda sat listening, dumbfounded, as Josie unburdened the private torment she had been shouldering all this time – from the money resting in the accounts in the First National Bank, the warning Max had left about Antonio Borelli, and the conversation she had with John Logan about Max fearing for his life.

"Sweetie," Linda began eventually, "have you considered perhaps the money might have something to do with Antonio Borelli?"

"What are you intimating, Linda, that Max was involved with organised crime?" Josie roared, immediately jumping to her feet.

Josie started pacing the room, she was conscious of the fact the words which had just leapt from Linda's lips were exactly the thoughts that had already entered her tortured mind, but hearing someone else say them out loud somehow made them more of a plausible reality.

Several agonising minutes later, Josie reached warily into her bag and withdrew the hidden floppy disk. "Annie gave this to me when we were alone; she said Max had given it to her for safe keeping. My instincts tell me it's got something to do with Antonio

Borelli – perhaps now's a good time to take a look."

Loading the disk onto Annie's machine, they were both intrigued, but fearful at the same time, as to the information it would divulge.

It took just a few agonising seconds before a list of contents materialised on the small screen. Coded headings had no meaning for the women, so Josie simply clicked on the first entry. Lists of names, bank account numbers, and money entries came into view before them again and again. Slowly, the women meticulously scanned the information they contained. The last entry, however, made them gasp with horror.

It held photo upon photo of men in somewhat compromising positions with scantily clad women or even, in a few cases, other men. The final few pictures sickened them to the core – the murder of a young blonde woman with a blood-splattered Antonio Borelli standing over her lacerated body, in his raised right hand a large-bladed knife. Trembling with the enormity of their discovery, Josie quickly ejected the disk from its internal place in the laptop.

"What do we do now?" Linda demanded, trying her best to hold herself together. Josie, still in shock, carefully slipped the damning evidence back in its case.

"Don't know about you, but I want to go home as soon as we can get a flight out. I don't feel safe here anymore." Relieved to hear the word home at last erupt from Josie's mouth, Linda agreed this was their only option. "But first, Linda, I should try and contact this Chief Inspector Wainwright and tell him about the disk."

"Yes that's a good idea, but just be careful; you won't know who you're talking to on the other end, we don't know who we can trust. Just don't say too much."

Josie eventually managed to find the number for New Scotland Yard and, after several attempts, was put through to the Chief Inspector's secretary.

"Good morning, how may I help you?"

Josie looked at her watch; yes of course it's morning in England. "Good morning, is it possible to speak to Chief Inspector Wainwright? Only, I have some information for him which I think will help him with a case."

"I'm sorry, the inspector is out of the office today, can anyone else help you?"

"No, thank you I'll call again tomorrow, will he be back then?"

"I'm sorry it's difficult to say, are you sure no one else can help you?"

"No, like I said, I'll ring back tomorrow, goodbye," Josie put down the receiver. "Shit Linda, he's not there."

"Bugger, I really don't think we should tell anyone else, Josie, like I said we don't know who we can trust."

"Ok, we need to find a secure place to hide this polluted disk," Josie pointed out before adding, "and Linda, I would like a chance to say goodbye to Annie properly by going back to the farm tomorrow as we planned, but only if that's ok with you though?"

"I have to say I'm not totally happy about leaving the apartment Josie, but I know you and Annie have a lot more to talk about, so yes, it's alright with me on one proviso: we try and change our flights to Saturday."

Neither of them slept well that night. Settling

down under the single sheet that simply protected her modesty, Josie reached for the photo of her daughters, tenderly positioned on the bedside table. Kissing the image in the silver frame fondly, as she had done every night since they left England, it suddenly dawned on her that, like the picture on the grand piano, this innocent portrait might be an appropriate place to hide the disk.

The following morning, they rose early and decided to pack their bags in preparation for their premature departure; in the event they did stay at Annie's for the night, they filled their small backpacks with overnight items. Sorting through her belongings, Linda came across the boomerang John had generously given her and for some unknown reason decided to leave it in her backpack.

Now able to discuss openly the situation which had shrouded her for so long, Josie had a heart to heart with Linda as they drove hell for leather towards Halfway Farm – neither of them daring to contemplate the whereabouts of the Borelli brothers.

"Linda, it pains me to consider the idea that Antonio had something to do with Max's death. But knowing now he's wanted for murder, I do feel more strongly than ever before that Max's death was not an accident."

Sadly, Linda agreed with her. Her head whirling with events that had occurred since that fateful day, she shared her thoughts with Josie. "Do you think Antonio knows about the existence of the disk and, if so, perhaps that was the reason he got in touch with you?" Josie was of the same mind; Linda's reasoning was unfortunately making sense. "And what of those men who seemed to be following us?" Linda added, now on a roll. "Had they been sent by Antonio to keep an eye on us do you think?"

Continuing their journey, further anxiety was building up relentlessly – after today, all they wanted to do was get back to their loved ones. They decided that, when they were ready to leave they would phone their families – making up some excuse as to why they were returning home early without alarming them. Josie would go straight to New Scotland Yard as soon as they landed to hand the disk directly to Chief Inspector Wainwright.

Yes, they would definitely feel better when that little evil article was out of their hands. With so much to occupy them, they were oblivious to the silver car once again on their tail; this time the driver and his passenger were both quite determined not to let them out of their sight again.

The road to the estate seemed longer than they remembered. As Halfway Farm came into view, Josie was moved with the thought this could be the last time she encountered Max's home; his youth, his past. Annie came out to greet them as before, but this time she suggested they park the car in the barn out of the unseasonable searing heat. Back in the comfort of the house, with more of the delicious homemade lemonade to cool them, they settled down to talk.

"John not around?" Linda queried, her dried lips appreciating the moist liquid from her now almost empty glass.

"He'll be back after lunch; he went to see his girlfriend last night in Cairns and stayed over as usual." Annie smiled as she contemplated her son's happiness at finding such a wonderful girl without any of the prejudices that had dominated her life. "By the way, I had an interesting phone call today from a woman enquiring into trekking who said you'd recommended us, Josie?"

"Woman, what woman? I've not spoken to anyone other than Linda about the farm." Alarm bells were ringing. "Did this woman leave her name?" Josie asked.

"No, she just said she had met you the other day and you had enthused about us," replied Annie, feeling slightly uneasy.

"Sorry Annie, but I've not mentioned the farm to anyone and anyway, I didn't know it existed as a business until yesterday."

Linda pulled out the newspaper from her bag and handed it to Josie. "I think Annie needs to know, Josie, don't you?"

Where to begin? Annie sat motionless as Josie divulged everything she and Linda knew about Max and the Borelli family.

"So let me get this straight. You think Max was murdered by these criminals and they're after you? Surely, you can't think they would have followed you half way around the world? How would they know you were coming here?" True. How could they have known about their arrangements? They certainly never mentioned to Antonio about visiting Australia when they met him at the pub, for one thing they hadn't planned to go then. So how on earth...?

"Josie," Linda cried, suddenly remembering, "didn't you tell me there was something wrong with your phone? Say it had been bugged, they could have heard all about our trip if that was the case."

"Shit, you could be right. You see it on films all the time. I've had another horrible thought; what about Tracey, Linda? You know, the girl at the travel agency. Remember how her manager got angry about her telling us of other people booking tickets for Australia?" Josie was beginning to let her imagination run away with her. "God, perhaps it was Antonio Borelli, or even his brother, perhaps the manager is part of the gang too."

The unexpected droning sound of a car engine rapidly approaching the house stopped their conversation in mid-flow. They watched nervously as a large black vehicle drew up in front of the building and the occupants stepped out into the strong morning sunlight. The women held their breath in anticipation from their hiding place beyond the curtained window. Both Linda and Josie gasped in horror as they immediately recognised three familiar faces: Antonio Borelli and the honeymooners.

"God, Linda," Josie whispered, "I know you were joking when you said they were our stalkers, but hell, you were right, they must have been tracking us all this time."

The emerging presence of the fourth occupant caused Linda to tremble violently from head to toe – the devil from her nightmares who had tried to rape her all those years ago was once again sharing the same continent as her, and breathing the same balmy air. The repugnant being she knew simply as Marco, was, she now realised, Marco Borelli.

CHAPTER 20 – THE MEN FROM HOME

Without any discussion, Annie threw back the multi-coloured rug covering the foot of the stairs. "Help me," she whispered urgently, tugging at the trap door neatly encased in the wooden floorboards. Springing to her aid, together they managed to lift the heavy entrance to the dark space below. "Quickly, the steps will lead you down to the basement; don't forget to take your backpacks so you don't leave any evidence you were here." Josie and Linda gave her a look of alarm. "Go on, don't argue! There's a light switch to the left as you go down. A door at the rear will take you out to the field at the back. If you're careful, you can make your way to the entrance behind the barn. It leads into the tack room, there's another door to the right into the main part of the barn, you should be able to get to your car from there – go, before they find out you're here!" Just as Annie replaced the carpet, she was aware of unwanted footsteps arriving outside her front door.

Slipping on the chain, she cautiously pulled the door ajar slightly to reveal a leggy young girl standing before her. "Annie?" the girl asked politely. Annie nodded. "I rang earlier; we're acquaintances of Josie, Josie Forrester."

"I remember," returned Annie, noting the men were still beside their car. "I did say there wouldn't be another trek until tomorrow, I'm afraid you've had a wasted journey." Praying she had ended the conversation, Annie tried to close the door but the girl managed to wedge her foot between it and the frame.

"Wasted? I think not. Do you live here alone, Annie?" The tone in her voice had changed and the look in her eyes sent a chill through Annie, who contemplated her answer for just a split second. John, her beloved son, would be returning soon but she wasn't about to reveal that fact to this unsettling stranger invading her home, so she lied in the hope they would all go away.

"I'm expecting a trek of about twenty people back at any minute." Unfortunately, the girl wasn't fazed by this disclosure.

"I see," she responded, sounding unconvinced. "Do you mind if we have a look around? I just adore horses; they're such magnificent, powerful creatures, aren't they?"

Annie was swift to reply. "Yes, as a matter of fact I do. I have several mares in foal at the moment, and I don't want them to be disturbed." However, Annie's pleas were to no avail: the girl removed her foot from the door, turned, and re-joined her male companions and following a brief conversation, the small group spread out and began a thorough search of the farm. Annie closed the door again and made sure the chain was still secure before leaping for the phone – only to find the line was dead.

***

Down in the basement, Linda and Josie began feeling their way around the dark, underground room. Finding the light switch, Linda flicked it on. When their eyes had adjusted to the dim light, they noticed their surroundings were filled with old furniture, relics from the farm's past.

"Linda, I'm scared, those men want to kill us; if they do, my girls will have lost both parents. I'm so sorry for getting you into this mess," Josie groaned as tears formed in her eyes.

"Look sweetie, those bastards haven't got us yet." She took Josie's hand in hers and squeezed it gently. "And anyway, they want that disk remember; they'd be stupid to kill us before they find out where it is. I need you to be strong. Don't forget we survived the Blue Mountains, didn't we?"

Josie managed to pull herself together and dried her tears. "Look over there, by that old bookcase," she whispered, suddenly pointing to a small door in the wall, "it must be the exit to the field."

It took all their efforts to turn the rusting key and handle, before pushing the weighty door which seemed to squeal with pain as its hinges grated together. They stopped and listened before continuing, hoping the unwanted intruders had not heard the clamour. Emerging into the dazzling daylight, they felt terrifyingly defenceless, like vulnerable prey waiting for their predators to pounce.

This time, Josie took the lead. With immense caution, lest they be discovered, they made their way stealthily to the rear of the barn, where they came across another small entrance and – just as Annie had described it – it opened into a tack room. Grabbing hold of the handle to the door on the right, Josie was taken aback when it wouldn't open – obviously something heavy was blocking it.

"Can you see what it is, Josie?" Linda asked softly,

frustrated at the thought of freedom, now almost within their grasp, being denied them.

Josie swivelled round to face Linda. "I think it's our ruddy car, we must have driven up to the door!"

"Bugger! Of all the luck, what the hell do we do now? Those bastards won't give up until they find us." Linda covered her eyes with her hands. Up until now, she had been the strong one, and had all the answers, but she seemed to be rapidly running out of ideas. She realised they had finally found themselves in a situation where there was literally no way out. Appreciating the feel of Josie's hand on her shoulder, she looked directly at her best friend. "I love you, Josie, whatever happens, I'm not sorry we came on this trip."

The unnerving sound of the barn door being flung open brought their conversation to an abrupt halt as the unseen intruders approached their vehicle.

"It's their bloody car; the bitches must be here somewhere – hiding like fucking rats. This must mean they know we're after them!"

"You're sure it's their car, Tony?" growled Antonio, trying hard to open the driver's door without any success.

"Positive, Cat and I've definitely been following this crappy motor for days."

"Well, you've never had any trouble with breaking into a car, cousin, now is your time to show me how it's done." With great satisfaction, Tony managed to gain entry into the driver's side, just as Marco and Cat joined the party.

"So it seems the bitches are on the run, I like that thought. I love the chase. I love the capture and, even more, I love the outcome," Marco drooled, his eyes focused on Cat.

"Marco, I've had about enough from you, keep your fucking eyes off my bird. Do you understand? She's not yours for the taking. Just keep your fucking eyes off her," roared Tony.

"Oh, my little cousin thinks he's a big man at last, don't worry I've got my eyes fixed firmly elsewhere, on a more, let's say, mature woman."

From the room next door, Josie and Linda shuddered at his depraved words.

Backing down from the hostile youth before him, Marco sniggered, satisfied. "I think it's time we had a proper talk to the Aboriginal woman, perhaps have a bit of fun, what do you say bro?"

"You'll get your fun later, Marco. We're here for the disk, just focus on the fucking disk. Keep your wandering hands to yourself and your trousers zipped," Antonio warned his brother. "We find the disk and leave no evidence behind us, do you all understand? I've no intention of rotting in a bloody jail!" Agitated, he turned to Tony. "Get the guns from the car."

In shock at the potential violence before them, Linda motioned to Josie to make their way back to Annie. Reaching the house, they re-entered the basement.

"Annie, Annie, can you hear us?" Josie called from the tomb below.

"Yes, didn't you get to your car?" she called back softly.

"Yes but it was parked against the door. Look, you have to get out of there. They've got guns and they know we're around here somewhere. We can't let you get hurt for us, Annie. Please, get out now!"

Too late. With great force, the front door was kicked open and the four felons stormed into the house.

"Well, Annie," snarled Antonio, as Marco and Tony easily overpowered her and forced her into a chair. "I think you know exactly who we are, don't you?" Annie's stony face revealed nothing. "I have a question for you," Antonio went on. "When was the last time you saw Max Forrester? Think carefully now, I don't want you to make my brother here angry, you really wouldn't like to see him angry!"

Annie could hardly speak, she was so petrified of the beings before her. The feeling of helplessness took her back to her childhood, when beatings were a regular occurrence. Marco's fingerless hand was now resting on her shoulder; he let out a soft groan as, very slowly, he began sliding it down into her buttoned blouse – seeking out her soft breast below.

"I haven't seen Max for twenty years," she whimpered.

"Now now, we happen to know you saw him recently," Antonio scolded as he leaned towards Annie, their faces almost touching. "STOP FUCKING LYING, BITCH! Why did he come here, what did he want?" Antonio was running out of patience. "I don't want to leave Marco alone with you; he's not the nicest of men where women are concerned."

In absolute terror, Annie finally responded to the threats and screamed. "He came to see his son, ok?"

Josie, who thought she had heard it all, was struck dumb in disbelief. What did she just hear Annie say? John was Max's son? No, surely not! Linda put an arm of comfort around her best friend.

"So, Max had a son! He didn't come here to leave you anything then? Perhaps something he wanted you to look after for him, say a disk maybe?"

"No, I told you, he came to see his son," Annie confirmed. Realising, uneasily, that the women waiting underneath the floorboards had heard this disclosure, she deeply regretted Josie had to hear the news in such a way.

"So where are Josie and her friend? We know they're here somewhere, we've seen their car in the barn."

Annie thought rapidly. "They went for a walk."

"A walk?" queried Antonio.

"Yes, they wanted to take pictures of the place before they left." Antonio was not convinced, believing Annie was lying.

"Marco, we're not going to get anything else from her, take the bitch around the back and deal with her. If she did have the disk, she's probably already got rid of it somehow. We'll go and search for the other two."

"Can I go with Marco, Antonio? I've not seen him kill before, it would be such a turn on," Cat begged, purring with excitement.

"You're fucking coming with me. Keep your horny ideas to yourself, woman," bellowed Tony, grabbing her around the waist and kissing her hard on the lips. "Keep it warm for me; I'll see you right when all this is over." This seemed to satisfy Cat, who kissed her lover back just as intensely.

Realising there was no time to waste, Josie and Linda left their prison under the house and found their way out again to the field at the back, where Marco was dragging his very reluctant victim. Arriving well before Annie and her depraved captor, they manoeuvred themselves behind the hut from which John had produced the highly decorated boomerang the day before.

All too soon, Marco arrived with the traumatised Annie – shotgun in hand. Snarling very close to her ear, he warned, "After sex, my next obsession is human-hunting, but I'm giving you a chance, only a slim one, you understand. Ready, steady, go, bitch!" He released his hold on Annie and she started running for her life towards the dense forest. Marco raised the shotgun to his shoulder and took aim.

They couldn't just stand by and watch Annie being murdered in front of them. Linda knew her little gadget wouldn't help them this time; no, she needed a weapon. Withdrawing from her backpack the gift John had presented her, she drew back her arm and with great force liberated the curved object into the windless air.

Circling the field with great precision, the boomerang rounded on Marco before he understood the implication, knocking him to the ground at the exact moment his finger pulled on the deadly trigger, firing its cartridge before it left his grasp. Unfortunately for Marco, the shortened barrel changed direction as it fell, mercifully not killing Annie but instead shooting its master high in the groin.

Linda stood, looking down with some satisfaction at the animal that had caused such pain and destruction to so many women's lives. Unconscious and bleeding, they left him lying in a pool of his own blood.

The booming sound of the shotgun had not only

reached the ears of Marco's companions, but it had also vibrated around the valley, sending startled creatures running for cover. There was urgency now for the encroaching unseen groups of individuals, who had been encircling the vast area for some time. The rays from the sun reflected off the professional police guns trained on Halfway Farm.

Instinctively, Annie felt it – the calm before the storm. "Let's get back into the basement. They think I'm dead, but it won't be too long before they come looking for Marco."

They dropped down beneath the house again; to listen, to wait. In the basement, where they knew their voices could not be heard, Annie spoke anxiously, "John will be home soon, if he's hurt ..."

Josie stopped her in her tracks. "So, John is Max's son? Why didn't you tell me?"

"What good would it have done? His father is dead; I simply didn't want to hurt you anymore."

All of a sudden, they were aware of raised voices outside. The next few minutes seemed like hours as unexpected, sporadic firing began overhead, and then as quickly as it had started, silence – a deadly silence.

They huddled together for comfort for several minutes, petrified at the unseen drama taking place outside, until, that is, they heard a joyous sound: a raised Australian voice vibrating thought the musty airways. "I'll look in the house, chief." Someone with heavy boots strode purposefully across the floor, causing dust to filter down through the cracks to the excited women below.

"Annie, do you think it's the police?" Josie asked.

"I think it could be, but let's wait until we're sure."

Just then, another person entered the house. "Any

sign of the women, sergeant? Only I want to get those killers to the station as soon as possible; won't be happy until they're behind bars."

"We're in the basement!" they chorused.

Slowly, the door to freedom lifted and the very welcome faces of the Australian Police Force looked down at them, offering assistance. Stepping gratefully out onto the porch, the sight of their three pursuers lying handcuffed on the ground met their eyes. It was over. They embraced each other and cried together – thanking God they had all survived.

"Have you been hurt?" the police chief enquired, concerned with the image before him of the three women covered in a cocktail of dirt and blood.

"No, we're all fine," Annie responded, brushing herself down as best she could, "but you'll find an injured man in the field at the back."

"Don't worry, we've got Marco Borelli. He's not going anywhere."

"How did you know they were here?" Linda began, as the silver car that had been trying hard to keep them under close surveillance approached the house, its occupants delighted to see their quarry safe and well. Alighting from their vehicle, the two weary English detectives smiled broadly with relief at the sight of the women, whose welfare had been entrusted to them by Chief Inspector Wainwright.

Glancing back up the drive, Annie caught sight of John's car hurtling towards her. "Mum, they wouldn't let me near the house, are you ok? I heard the shooting. Mum, are you ok?" John roared, sweeping his mother off her feet, while his dogs barked wildly around her.

"I'm ok now, John, honestly I am, a little shaken,

but ok. At least, I will be after a long bath." Annie cried, remembering the revulsion she felt when Marco invaded her body. She turned to Linda, emotion in her eyes with the realisation of all they had been through. "There was a moment ... but Linda here saved my life, for which I will always be eternally grateful."

Gradually, the sound of a horse's hooves thundering down the drive reached their ears. Scott Jones, riding wildly in his saddle, reined back hard to bring his exhausted mount to a sliding halt in front of Annie, sending a cloud of dust high into the air. Dismounting quickly, he took Annie passionately in his arms, vowing never to leave her again.

More vehicles made their steady way down the tree-lined drive. One stopped a few yards before the house. An unexpected, familiar figure climbed out, eager to shower Josie with love. With her heart pounding hard in her chest, Josie ran towards him wailing, "Dad? Dad, is it really you?"

David gathered his treasured daughter safely to him. "Josie, my beloved girl, did they harm you? I should never forgive myself if they touched you."

"I'm fine, dad, Linda's fine, and Annie; well ... it could have been a lot worse. But how...? Why are you here?"

"I told you all those years ago that if you ever needed me I'd be there and, well, here I am ... Josie, listen darling, I've got something important to tell you."

"Is it mum? I know she hasn't been well lately, is it mum, dad?"

David spoke softly to sooth her anxiety. "No darling, it's not mum."

Gently, he turned his daughter around. Gazing out through the shimmering heat, she perceived walking hesitantly towards her the figure of a man: a tall broad-shouldered man with deep blue eyes, his hair now streaked with a touch of grey.

"Josie, my dearest Josie, I'm so sorry," sobbed a very remorseful Max, as she collapsed into his waiting arms.

CHAPTER 21 – LOVE IS ALL YOU NEED

Cautiously Josie opened her eyes; the face of her dad gradually came into focus. David had been sitting diligently by her bedside, holding her hand, ever since they arrived at the small hospital following her abrupt collapse at the farm.

"How long have I been here, dad?" Josie began weakly; she was still feeling a little groggy from the injection the doctor had administered. "Where's Linda, is she ok?" she asked, looking anxiously around the room while trying to ease herself out of bed; a move she soon gave up on as the lower part of her body still seemed partially asleep.

"Now, the doctor said you need to rest, pumpkin, so just lie back for a little bit longer darling, please. To answer your question, you've been here over twelve hours. Linda's well, all things considered. They've just gone to get a coffee."

"Dad, you called me pumpkin, you've not called me that since I married Max."

"You'll always be my little girl, Josie. Darling, do you remember what happened yesterday?

Josie deliberated carefully for a minute. "I remember the sound of shooting. They got them, didn't they? Antonio Borelli and the others?" She cried, rising again from her pillow, unnerved suddenly by the thought of Antonio still being out there, ruthlessly hunting them down; his gun at the ready with the sole intention of putting an end to their lives.

"Yes, you've nothing to be worried about. They've been taken to Cairns Police Station."

Reassured by her father's words, she began to recall the period after the gunfire had ceased. "After that, things are a bit of a blur, I remember seeing you. Oh, how wonderful it was to see you." Josie squeezed his hand fondly. "Then I think I must have been hallucinating. If I say it out loud, dad, you'll think I'm going mad." She closed her eyes tightly, fearful of the words she was about to relay. "Dad, I think I saw ... Max, but I couldn't have, could I, dad? He's dead, Max is dead!"

Linda and Annie appeared just then, clutching four mugs of lukewarm coffee from the hospital canteen. They were overjoyed to see Josie awake at last, and hugged her so tight she thought she would pass out again. However, having overheard Josie's last comment, Linda looked at her friend uneasily – the realisation that her husband was, in fact, still alive had not yet registered; it was going to be very traumatic for her to try to grasp.

"We're all going home tomorrow, if you feel like travelling?" Linda announced. "Chief Inspector Wainwright has pulled a few strings, we're going first class!"

"Chief Inspector Wainwright, is he here too? That's why I couldn't get hold of him; he must have already been on his way here."

"Yes, he accompanied your dad and ... please try to understand sweetie, Max ... is still alive. He's waiting outside to see you, he doesn't want to upset you ... but he is desperate to explain."

Josie felt her whole body quiver. So it was true; she

hadn't dreamt it. Without uttering a single word, she nodded acknowledgment in Linda's direction.

Slowly the room cleared and a face she had fantasised about so many times over the past year appeared before her – the face of her husband, looking tired and drawn. Steadily, Josie eased her aching body down from her hospital bed and for a long, long time they stood, simply looking into each other's eyes, as if in a trance.

Warily, Max reached out towards her, affectionately taking hold of both her hands in his, kissing them tenderly. He pulled her closer so their bodies, which yearned for the close intimacy they once knew, came together again. He kissed away the tears tumbling freely down her cheeks and the sweet trembling lips he had dreamt about for so long.

"Max, you bloody bastard," she suddenly shrieked, breaking away from him. "Kissing me isn't going to eradicate the agony you've put me and the girls through for the past year, how could you let us believe you were dead?

"Josie I'm so sorry, I didn't set out to hurt you, believe me, things just got out of hand. Give me a chance to explain, please just give me a chance."

"Ok." She sat back down on the bed. "What happened in Castle Street? The body, who was it, Max?" He was relieved, at last, to have the chance to explain everything to her.

He began at the very beginning – with his encounter with Antonio in the park. Little by little, his sorry story unfolded. Max emphasised how ashamed and disgusted he felt with the perilous situation he had got himself into and how he had tried to find a way out so his family would be safe. Finally reaching the point in time where he had arranged to meet Antonio in the café off Castle Street, Josie stirred uncomfortably as she remembered her emotions on that unforgettable day.

Max described waiting nervously for Antonio at the table by the window and, in order to justify keeping his vantage point, he felt obliged to drink mug after mug of tea. After a period of time, when Antonio had still not appeared, he foolishly left his coat and briefcase where he had been sitting so he didn't relinquish his seat, in desperation for the bathroom. When he returned to his table, both his coat and briefcase were missing.

A loud screeching of brakes and the screams of a woman outside caused him and the other customers to rush out onto the pavement. Situated halfway up a fog-encased Castle Street lay the distorted body of a man, an unfortunate thief who was in the wrong place at the wrong time. From his concealed position amongst the growing crowd of onlookers, Max witnessed someone picking up his leather briefcase, which had been discarded several metres from the body. Turning his face briefly in Max's direction, Max realised it was Antonio removing the damaged disk from its torn shell.

It rapidly dawned on him that Antonio thought it was him lying there on the narrow street with his bones crushed and broken. It was at this precise moment Max made up his mind to disappear, to ultimately put an end to the potential trouble he had brought his family; at least, that is what he convinced himself.

Going over the event in his head repeatedly over the months that followed, Max believed the lorry was probably driven by one of Antonio's delivery drivers, who had been waiting for him to leave the café before driving up Castle Street and because of the poor visibility that day, had wrongly assumed it was him. He was sure Antonio would have enticed the man to drive up the narrow street with the incentive of a very large bonus in his pay packet.

Steadily absorbing everything Max was telling her, Josie got up from the bed and looked at her husband, her eyes full of fury.

"How could you possibly believe that pretending you were dead was a good idea? Did you not contemplate, for one moment, the suffering you were about to inflict on the girls and me? You selfish pig!" Josie yelled, pounding on his chest, punishing him for all the days and nights she had cried for him. Max just stood still, taking her outrage, knowing it was only what he deserved.

Afraid she would collapse again, he finally lowered her back onto the bed. "Josie, the men I was dealing with were pure evil. I had seen exactly what they were capable of: disgusting, depraved acts, even on people they supposedly loved." Thinking of Candy, Max dropped his voice. "Pictures which will haunt my dreams forever, I seriously couldn't have lived with myself if I was the cause of anything like that happening to you and the girls, that's why I left. I thought I was doing the right thing; please believe me, darling, I honestly thought I was doing the right thing."

Josie managed to compose herself and looked him straight in the eyes, trying to digest his reasoning; after all, she too had been privy to the nauseating scenes on the disk, she too was finding it impossible to eradicate the images from her mind.

"Ok Max ... what happened after you made the decision to flee, to leave me and the girls? Where did you go?"

Resuming his story, he explained that fortuitously he had money in his pocket; his idea was to make his way down to Devon, to stay in David and June's bungalow, which, of course, he knew would be empty. Finding the key June always hid under the pot below the front bedroom window, he let himself in. He stayed there alone for many weeks, eating the food from the cupboards – which he had fully intended on replacing – leaving no trail of his visit.

When David and June surprised him by arriving early to open up for the summer, he made his departure quickly through the French doors. Taking the bicycle from the shed, he bummed around the south of the country doing casual jobs as he went, biding his time until the weather started its winter chill.

Back once again at the bungalow, he made the painful decision to leave England and his beloved family and go back to Australia. He realised, of course, he couldn't get out of the country without his passport, therefore he had no other option but to return to Willow Green. To his despair, he found the locks on the doors of Brook Cottage had been changed. Not wanting to arouse suspicion by breaking into his home, he decided he had no choice but to go back to Devon and think of another plan.

Josie became even more distressed at the thought he had been so near. "We actually had a break in soon after you ... died. That's why I had to get the locks changed. Thinking about it now, it must have been

Antonio and Marco looking for the second disk."

"You're probably right, Antonio would have realised I had made another copy. I did see you though, while I was there, I followed you for several days. I watched from the shadows of an old oak tree as you and the girls stood by my graveside on the anniversary of my death. How I wished I could have left my hiding place and run up to you, shout from the top of my voice that I was still alive and everything was going to be all right again. I knew it was impossible, it would have meant putting you in the line of danger I had been trying my best to avoid, and everything I had done up to then would have been for nothing." Max sighed despondently, recalling that particular moment and how he was forced to simply disappear back into the morning mist.

"Reluctantly, I hitch-hiked back to the bungalow, where I must have begun to feel a bit too relaxed in my surroundings because I was fast asleep in what I've always considered to be our room when I was suddenly jolted awake by your mother's hysterical screams. It was quite a bombshell for all of us, I can tell you. After your dad managed to calm her down and they had both got over the shock, we sat talking into the night, agreeing not to tell anyone else that I was alive, mainly because to come clean would just be too dangerous for all concerned. The following day, your dad phoned to make excuses for you and the girls not to come down to the bungalow – I knew he hated lying to you, but he had no choice."

At last, the past year was beginning to make sense. "So what made you and dad travel here? I mean, thank god you did, I'm not sure we would still be alive."

Max leaned over towards her, he couldn't stop himself from kissing her again. "Your mum and dad saw the piece in the newspaper about the arrest of the Borelli family when they were in France and came rushing back to tell me."

"So the girls know you're alive?"

Max grinned, recalling the shocked, ecstatic faces of Beth and Emma. "They certainly do. I knew then I had no choice but to give myself up; I was convinced Antonio assumed you knew the whereabouts of the second disk and was probably following you so I went to see Chief Inspector Wainwright. What a surprise that was. He told me he had men trailing you because they had known for some time I had an association with the Borelli family. Not only that, he knew right from the beginning that it wasn't my body in Castle Street, but as he pointed out, I was just a small fish in a very large pond. The police were sure Antonio and Marco had been monitoring your movements by putting a tap on your phone, knew you had left the country, and were probably heading for Cairns after you. It took a bit of persuading from your dad and me to convince them to let us accompany them out here instead of just locking me up. Then, since I was registered as a dead man, we had to arrange for another passport."

A knock at the door caused them both to look up as Chief Inspector Wainwright apologised for the intrusion. "I wonder if you feel up to answering a few questions, Mrs. Forrester?" Climbing from the bed, Josie sat with the inspector, relating all she knew. "So where is this disk now, Mrs. Forrester?"

"It's with my things in the apartment."

Max pointed to the bags in the corner of the room.

"Linda's finished your packing for you, it's all there."

Grasping the frame containing the picture of their daughters, Josie carefully opened the back and handed the damning evidence to the inspector, verification of the evil surrounding Antonio and Marco, which would without doubt put the brothers away for a very long time.

"Can we come back in now?" cried Linda and Annie, appearing around the door, desperate to join their two friends in order to play their part in the reunion.

"Yes, I've finished for the time being," confirmed the inspector. "But obviously when we return to the UK there will be further questions to be answered from all of you."

"What about Max, what will happen to him? I've only just got him back, are you going to take him away from his family again, inspector?"

"Josie," intervened Max. "I already know the answer. I'll be arrested as soon as we set foot back in the UK; I've been involved with criminals, unfortunately the police have no choice."

"But you helped catch them Max, without that disk..."

"Mrs. Forrester, all I can tell you at this juncture is the evidence Max has collected has been of great use. I will do all in my power to support him when his case comes up in court. I'm afraid I can't say any more."

It was with mixed feelings they reached Cairns Airport on Sunday afternoon for their flight home. Annie and John were there to wave them goodbye. Max and Josie promised they would be back some day, but next time they would bring the girls with them to meet their brother. Settling down into their first class seats, Josie looked over at Max, who was beginning to look relaxed at last.

She knew there were still enormous hurdles to climb, that he would certainly face charges when he got home, but after all they had been through, it was a small price to pay. She had her beloved husband back, the girls had their father; they would eventually be a family again.

What a reception they had when they landed at Heathrow Airport. Everyone was there to greet them – June, Emma, Beth, Patrick, Richard, and several members of the police force, all relieved to see them safely home. The Borelli gang and their police companions had arrived the previous day in handcuffs, three of them having been whisked away immediately to their small grey-walled cells, in which they would no doubt be spending a very long time. However, Marco, still in pain, had been driven away in a waiting ambulance under armed guard.

"Mum," cried Emma and Beth together as they suddenly caught sight of Josie striding towards them amongst the other passengers, "we've missed you, mum."

"Not as much as I've missed you, darlings," Josie shrieked, gathering her daughters in her arms. Turning to June, she exclaimed, "Mum, oh mum, for a while I wondered if I would ever see any of you again."

"Josie dear, you've had quite an adventure. Let's get home, you can tell us all about it over a nice cup of tea."

"Oh mum, thank you for being you." And for the first time in years, she kissed her.

Hiding behind a large bouquet of flowers, a beaming Richard and Patrick stepped forward while Richard lifted Linda off her feet.

"Richard, the flowers are lovely, thank you and Patrick, my dear, wonderful boy, I'm so relieved to see you." She hugged her son, not wanting to let him go.

"Linda, fancy getting out of here and going somewhere for a quiet drink?" invited Richard.

"Go on mum, I'll go back with Beth and Emma, we'll have plenty of time later to catch up," encouraged Patrick. Linda looked apprehensive about leaving him again so soon. "It's fine, honestly mum; I'll see you back in Willow Green."

"If you're sure Patrick, then yes, yes please Richard."

Just as Max, David and Chief Inspector Wainwright arrived with the luggage, two burly police officers approached Max.

"Max Forrester, I'm arresting you for ...

"Max," screamed Josie.

"Josie, we knew this would happen, darling. Keep positive and remember I love you and the girls."

"Just a minute, officer. Max Forrester is in my custody, there's no need for handcuffs," pointed out the inspector, showing them his badge.

"Yes, of course, Chief Inspector, we were only carrying out orders."

"Max, I'm sorry but we do have to go now," apologised the inspector.

Full of emotion, Josie and her daughters watched, helplessly clinging to each other, as Max was escorted from the terminal building. Drawing comfort from Chief Inspector Wainwright's promise that the information Max had given the police would help in his judgement, she prayed he was a man of his word and would keep his promise, because Max Forrester was the love of her life.

EPILOGUE

The trial was newspaper headlines for months. The gruesome details of murder, rape and all the other evil acts that the Borelli's were responsible for became so predominant in all aspects of news reporting that Josie eventually refused to buy papers or listen to the television. Actually, she really had no need because she was there in person, sitting in the gallery with her father and Linda, while the prosecuting council was pulling Max and their lives apart, bit by bit, day after day.

Of course, there was no doubt in anyone's mind that the Borelli's were guilty and when the jury finally returned with that verdict, the courtroom erupted into mass hysteria. Life sentences, the judge pointed out in this case, meant life; there was definitely no chance that either Giorgio or his sons would ever be able to walk the streets again.

Tony was given ten years, while Cat just six. Her screams of injustice reverberated throughout the room, but not one person had any sympathy for the manipulative shrew. Max ... well, it was a relief to everyone when the judge granted him a suspended sentence. At last, he was able to return home to his family and friends a free man. The dawn of the twenty-first century was also the dawn of a new phase of all their lives.

***

"Yes, the invitation came in the post this morning. Yes, the girls will be round to yours this afternoon for a final fitting, and yes, Linda, everything will be wonderful. Stop panicking, I thought that was my job as chief bridesmaid."

It was the end of May, and Linda and Richard were getting married; it could not have been more of a romantic ending for Josie's best friend. Max had been home for over a month now and it would take time for them all to adjust, they understood that, but they had no doubt they would come through. In their hearts, they were incredibly happy; happier than they had ever dared hope they would be again.

"Aunty Linda, the cars are here," Beth called up the stairs in Brook Cottage on the morning of the joyful day. Brenda was putting the final touches to Linda's hair and makeup.

"Are you ready, Linda? Wow, you really look beautiful, this dress was definitely the right choice."

After months of searching, Linda had finally found the most delicate cream lacy dress imaginable. "I don't know if I've ever told you, but thank you for everything; for always being there for me, I couldn't have got through all these years without you." Josie whimpered.

"Don't, you'll make me cry, can't let my mascara run now. Brenda, can I just have a moment with Josie please? Josie, I hope we'll always be friends. I love you, sweetie, like a sister."

"I love you too. Come on then, sis, there's a handsome man waiting for you; you don't want to be late."

***

The white limousine drew up in front of the registry office and Linda and David stepped out into the morning sunlight. David had been thrilled when Linda asked him if he would give her away, her own dad being too ill to attend. There they all were, her three bridesmaids dressed in lilac, waiting and smiling at the blushing bride.

"Not too late to back out," Josie teased.

"Josie, I can't wait to be Mrs. Blake. Come on everyone, let's go in."

Walking in step behind the bride, Josie couldn't help but remember her own wedding day and how ecstatically happy she had felt. The years since then had been turbulent; no question about it, but now the future that loomed out ahead of them seemed brighter than ever; a future with Max, her partner in life.

Reaching the place where Richard was standing in front of the registrar's table, Linda handed her bouquet to Josie, who smiled at her friend before taking her place beside Max. Beaming at the sight of his wife, Max leaned over and kissed Josie softly. Yes, her life was truly wonderful.

THANK YOU!

To my Reader:

Many thanks for buying *All For the Love of Josie*, I hope you enjoyed reading it.

If you did enjoy it, please post a review at Goodreads or your favourite social network site and let your friends know about *All For the Love of Josie*.

Look out for more stories from *Willow Green* coming soon.

Happy Reading!
All the best
Evelyn

CONTACT DETAILS

Like on Facebook: facebook.com/1evelynharrison

Cover designed by: www.StunningBookCovers.com

Published by: Raven Crest Books
www.ravencrestbooks.com

Follow us on Twitter:
www.twitter.com/lyons_dave

Lightning Source UK Ltd.
Milton Keynes UK
UKOW01f1026230715

255694UK00006B/80/P